Release My Heart

Leigh Armstrong

Leigh Armstrong

To my husband, David
Thank you for all you do,

For your love and support,

And for all that is ahead of us.

I love you with all my HEART!

Leigh Armstrong

Cover Design by Philip Andrews Photography

Editing by Amy Elizabeth Bishop

Contact Information for Leigh Armstrong

Website: www.leigharmstrong2018.com

Email: leigharmstrong2018@yahoo.com

Instagram/Facebook/Goodreads

Printed in the United States of America

First Print May 2019

ISBN: 978-1-7326939-1-3 Paperback

Contents

Prologue

Michael

*J*ve been driving around for a while as my mind goes to places I didn't want it to go. My fear is that she's hurt or worse. Jamie never made it to the meeting with Stacey tonight. I know because I was there thirty minutes before they were to meet in the back booth.

I come to a four way stop, needing to go back when I notice an SUV pull up behind me. The rain is falling hard but I can see two people in the front seat who seem to be arguing. The driver is wearing a baseball cap and the passenger is pushing at the driver. My eye is drawn to the passenger, long hair waving back and forth when she pushes him forward. The hat falls off and I see his face.

Josh?

He reaches out, then slams her against the dashboard.

It's Jamie! Jamie!

I blow my horn, push the car in park, open the door, then run to them. She looks at me and in seconds screams my name, beating the dashboard, then smacking Josh. He notices my fist come at his face, though I hit the window instead. He punches the accelerator pulling away, but I hold on to the mirror. Even though I yell at him to stop, he speeds away with her.

Son of a bitch! Back in my car, I take off after them. *Where is she? I can't see her!* My heart pounds loudly in my chest. *My phone, where is my phone?* I glance up to see him push her against the passenger door. *What the hell?*

I blow my horn in hopes someone sees us and calls the police. A sign signals a curve up ahead and with the excessive speed, a wreck is imminent. As I come around the curve to continue my chase, I see the SUV sitting in the road. My foot slams on the brake, not wanting to crash into them. In seconds, I hit water, sending the car into a spin. I fight to hold onto the steering wheel, but the car flips so quickly, and lands inverted. The airbag inflates, slamming me back against the seat. It's disorienting, but I look for the SUV as lights move away from me. Unable to stop Josh and trapped in my car, I begin to beat, rip, or kick whatever to free myself. My chest feels tight and breathing becomes difficult.

Why is she with him, where is he taking her?

Chapter 1

Jamie

I wake to find myself in a dimly lit room with boxes stacked around me. The floor is concrete, and the ceiling is high with exposed metal beams, so I'm possibly in a warehouse. I blink my eyes several times, trying to clear my vision, and find my arms are tied to the chair I'm sitting in, along with my ankles. A bright light comes on overhead, stinging my eyes, but I open them to see a figure walking out of the darkness in front of me. I think back to the man with the black boots who attacked me at the apartment. As the person gets closer, I see they're the same. It's Josh…but why? And he's not alone; someone is behind him. A woman steps to the side and walks towards me. Dread comes over me as my body tightens. My hands form into fists, stretching the ties around them.

"Well look who decided to wake up," Stacey says. "How are you feeling, sweetie?"

She puts her hands inside her coat pockets eyeing me for a reaction, but I say nothing. I guess it's not what she wanted from me because her hand slaps my face, jerking my head violently to the side. I refuse to give her any kind of satisfaction of knowing how bad it hurt so I clench my teeth before responding.

"Did I get the meeting place wrong?"

"Cute, real cute."

I look at Josh. "Is she the woman you spoke about?"

He says nothing, but she walks to him, placing her hand on his chest. His eyes stay on me and I feel a sudden chill.

"Let me fill her in, lover." She kisses him. "We met at a bar with an instant attraction. We were inseparable. He'll do anything for me, just like I'll do anything for him. Isn't that right Josh?"

He touches her face. "I will."

"She's only using you," I tell him. "You said it yourself that she gets what she wants and doesn't care who she hurts. This is wrong. You don't have to do this."

She turns to me. "Honey, you have no idea what I am capable of doing when I set my mind to it. I have the most amazing story to tell you."

A chair is placed in front of me as she takes a seat.

"You and I have a few things in common. Let's start with our upbringing. I grew up bathed in money, the best private schools, and a new blue convertible when I turned sixteen. You had no money, public school, and an old pickup truck when you turned sixteen. I grew up in Texas, as you did. My mother was absent for most of my life, usually on pills or an alcoholic binge pining away over a lost love, whereas your mother was dead by the time you were five. My father was around but not aware of my activities, which opened so many opportunities to do whatever I wanted to whomever I wanted. Still have no idea? This is going to be the best part of the story. Let's start with my father's name—well, my biological father's name—first. Jamison Craig Morgan. He lived in Covington, Texas with his wife, Amanda. Ring a bell?"

"That's not true."

"It actually is true, and I have proof. Come on, little sis, play along. Okay, you know what our father looked like, so let me fill you in on my mother. She was a tall beautiful blonde with captivating blue eyes, admired by many I'm sure, except her husband. You see, their marriage was arranged, an agreement between two wealthy families who wanted an empire along with heirs. They obviously were not into it as much as their families were, so both became unhappy right away. They went outside the marriage to find love or lust. Your father—I mean, *our* father— was unhappy with your mother as well, so mine filled the void. You know the rest, adultery, lies and a pregnancy, blah, blah, blah. Are you following me? My mother would have been outed, shamed for her extramarital affair by the family, so she kept her secret from all of them, choosing wealth. My mother loved me only because I was the daughter of the man she loved. Sad, isn't it? My supposed father had no idea I was not his and he showered me with everything a girl could ever want, except for his time and discipline."

She stood, looking down at the floor.

"My mother was found in the horse barn from a supposed overdose, taking the secret with her. After the burial I went to her room--which was separate from my dads of course— looking around, maybe missing her. But what I found was a small box hidden in her closet with journals, detailing her feelings, their meetings, then me. I found no name for him, but she had a picture of her with some other buyers at one of the horse auctions." She pulls out a photo. "Look, do you see what I see?"

She holds it in front of me. I see six people, four men standing with two women. A blonde is standing next to my father and in the background is an old red truck. That truck sat in our barn for years until it was sold when I was fourteen.

"This means nothing."

She throws a tattered baby blanket at me; I used to have the missing corner.

"You helped me figure all this out without even knowing it. When Josh broke into your apartment, you helped me find out the truth. So really, you played an important part in hurting the man you now love. My name was changed when I turned 18. I left Texas, having my father sent to Italy after his unfortunate accident that left him unable to move or speak. So, you see little sis, I do make things happen. And now I want Michael."

"He's not yours to have. You sealed your fate with him."

"His family owns a multi-million dollar business, properties all over, and that's what I want. When I met him, he was a frat boy with a drinking

5

problem, Daddy issues, and a chip on his shoulder. We had something special, but you messed it all up."

"He'll never trust you because of what you've done."

"Shut up, just shut up!"

She stood up, clearly angered by my comment. I brace myself for another assault but instead she begins pacing in front of me. Then she stops, untying her coat and placing her hands on her stomach.

"Michael and I will always have a connection. That special night we spent together over Thanksgiving gave us a miracle. I'm pregnant with his baby."

I stare at her bulging stomach and tears sting my eyes at what I've just heard, but I know in my heart it's not true. They didn't sleep together that night. This is just more lies to get what she wants.

"I don't believe you."

"This baby is his. He'll accept him or her with open arms. I guess it's hard knowing the man you love slept with another woman and then got her pregnant. Sound familiar? But the difference is, I want him to be the father of this baby so that I can have all the things I want."

"No, you won't get away with this idiotic plan. He won't accept this without a fight."

She walks to the side of my chair. "I will have this baby, I will have Michael's support, and I will become part of his family. You'll only be a bad memory pushed out by this baby. Any loss he'll feel when you go missing will be replaced by his sweet child. So, I guess you could say, I win."

"This will blow up in your face. He loves me."

She raises her hand and I turn my face, waiting for the pain. Instead of hitting me this time, she pushes my chair over with her foot and my head bumps the floor. Pain rushes through it and my body aches from the jolt.

"Josh, pick her up."

He does as she asks. Our eyes meet. I look for something that could maybe give me hope, but his eyes hold nothing. He turns away from me after setting me upright.

"Let me finish. You're going to break his heart by just disappearing from existence. He'll be sad for a little bit, but as soon as I tell him about the baby, you won't matter anymore. Your life with him is over. Do you understand what I am saying?

"He knows I would never leave him. Not like this."

"You'll do as you are told, or I will destroy him by taking this baby away. Right now, I have people in place who are waiting for me to give the word to begin the downfall of his parents' business and bringing to light his father's extramarital affairs. Do you understand me? All this time you thought you had won, that I had rolled over without any fight in me, when what truly was happening was my plan of destroying your world. You can either leave on your own or I will be forced to get rid of you permanently. Taking a life to save myself was never hard before and you're just an insignificant blip to erase."

"You're crazy. He won't stop trying to find me and I won't ever let him go. I love him—he means more to me than my own life."

"Like I said, your life is nothing compared to getting my life where I want it. Josh, it's time."

He walks over, pulling on a pair of gloves.

"Josh, she'll get rid of you like she's trying to get rid of me," I say desperately. "You're not what she wants. Whatever she's promising you, it won't happen."

"It's already begun," he says.

"You're both crazy. You won't get away with any of this."

She turns to him. "Is everything set?"

"Yes."

"Good. Give me five minutes with my sister and then we will continue."

Josh walks away and she suddenly comes up, pulling me by my hair, and jerking my head back.

"Listen up. You won't be around to see Michael because if he doesn't take this pregnancy news and support me, I will end this pregnancy and your worthless body will wash up in the lake. Do you understand me?" She pulls my hair harder. "Answer me!"

I yell. "NO! I won't let you hurt him or anyone."

"You won't be able to help him, but he'll know it was you who caused the baby's death. When little things are left unattended, plans fall apart. I will not be weak like my mother. I'm in control of my future."

Josh returns. She lets me go and pulls her coat together, tying the belt. "Josh, are you ready?"

"Yes."

"Good. I'm leaving. Don't be late, baby." She kisses him in a way that makes my stomach turn. She leaves and he unties my hands. I fight against him, but he grabs my hands, squeezing my wrists.

"Jamie! Nothing you do can stop what's about to happen."

He ties my wrist together before loosening my ankles. He then picks me up over his shoulder, taking me to a black SUV. I beat his back with my tied hands, but he shoves me inside the vehicle. He's surprisingly stronger than I thought. The door slams once he's inside the vehicle and I struggle to pull myself back up again.

"Stop! No one is here. You won't be heard even if you scream."

"So, I'm supposed to let you take me away where I am to be what, forgotten, tortured, or killed? Josh, this isn't right. You can help, just let me go. I can tell the police you were forced, threatened, anything you want me to tell them. Michael won't ever accept the baby as his or stop looking for me. You know this."

"Look, you're only making it worse for him. She'll be at the next destination twenty minutes after me."

"She wants revenge. You'll become a problem, expendable."

His hands tighten on the steering wheel, twisting nervously as he drives. "She has people working with her. I have no choice."

"No, she'll kill you!"

"If you love Michael and want him to live, then you need to shut up and do everything she says."

"How long before she gets rid of me?"

"It's indefinite."

I'm now desperate as to what to do. He just said I was to be kept until she's assured Michael will be on board with accepting her and the baby. But then what?

I have to fight.

I turn my body to kick at him with all the anger that is inside of me, but he hits me and knocks me against the door.

"Jamie, enough. There is nothing that will change what's going to happen. There are measures in place already."

The hit is a blessing in disguise. As I'm knocked up against the door, I'm in a curved position, and somehow able to free the ties around my hands. I come back at him with all I have this time. It's raining hard and he swerves a few times, trying to fight me off when we come to stop at the edge of town. I push him into the steering wheel and that's when I notice Michael's car ahead of us. I begin screaming his name and banging on the dash, but Josh slams me forward, pinning me down but it doesn't stop me. Michael gets out and approaches the SUV when our eyes lock on each other. Josh jerks away as Michael's fist slams into the window, he then hits the accelerator, and we pull off. He's beating the SUV, screaming, trying to get Josh to stop. I look back to see him climb into his car and begin to follow us.

"Josh, please stop, pull over." I look behind us. "Please stop!"

"No, he saw us. I have to try and lose him."

We take the corner too fast, skidding around in the road from the standing water and come to an abrupt halt that throws me against the door. He grips the steering wheel.

"Now let's see what happens."

"If you stay here, he'll hit us head on."

Just then I see Michael coming straight for us. He turns the wheel to miss us, trying to dodge the same standing water, but he can't. His car veers off the side of the road, rolling over a few times to a sudden halt. I scream as Josh pulls away. Panic, fear, or adrenaline fuels me as I begin my assault, yanking at his hands on the steering wheel, which causes him to over correct and we run off the road, crashing into an embankment.

Chapter 2

Three weeks after Jamie's disappearance
Michael

My parents are concerned that my melt down in the bathroom may happen again, so they stay in town to watch over me, but also to help devise a plan of action to find Jamie. The past few weeks have left me not wanting to eat, drink, or sleep as all my efforts are concentrated on searching for her. I've not attended one class since her disappearance. The injuries I received from the accident didn't hurt as much as not knowing where she is. I sit on my bed seeing reminders of her around me, when I hear my mom's voice at my bedroom door.

"Michael, someone is here to see you." She hesitates. "It's Stacey."

I've not seen her since that night. She came to the hospital, but I refused to see her. I walk past my mom into the living room where I find Stacey standing, wearing a coat and holding her purse and a plant.

"Why in hell are you here?"

"Not the greeting I expected but you do look better." She sets down the plant. "This is for you and I have some news that might cheer you up."

"Only if it's about Jamie. Anything else and you can go."

She looks over at my mom. "Mrs. Tucker, could you excuse us? I have some information for Michael that is private."

My mother walks between us, giving me a concerned look. "Do you want me to leave?"

"No, you can stay—there's nothing private between us."

"It'll make sense when I tell you."

My head says kick her out, but I cling to any information that will help find Jamie. I touch my mom's arm.

"How about you get the mail."

She eyes Stacey. "I'll be back in five minutes."

Stacey walks over to the sofa, unbuttoning her coat. "She's protective of her son."

"What's the information?" I ask brusquely.

"You've been upset by Jamie's abrupt disappearance with your neighbor, but my news will make you feel better." She turns to me. "This is what happened the night of the party. We're going to have a baby."

The look on my face should have sent her running from the apartment, but it doesn't.

"This is not my child because we didn't sleep together that night and you know it."

"Look, it's a shock just as it was for me."

I back away. "Those pictures were staged. You drugged me and several of the other team members that night."

"That's crazy talk. I already told you I didn't. This baby will become the most important person in your life now."

"Did you tell Jamie you were pregnant?"

"No, of course not. I waited to tell you first."

"Did you know Josh, the guy Jamie was with that night?"

"No. I heard he was shot in the head. Could she be capable of doing something so horrible?"

"Jamie didn't shoot him!"

"Look, you have to accept she's gone."

"NO! That will never happen."

"You're going to be a father whether you are ready or not. I won't do this alone. We both know how an absent father affects a child. Please don't do this to our baby."

I can't be sure she didn't know Josh, nor can I be sure she didn't have something to do with Jamie's disappearance, but I need to buy some time to figure it all out. There is more to this situation than she is telling me. Everyone is a suspect until I find Jamie. So, I take a different approach.

"I need time to process this information."

I pick up her coat, handing it to her. She slips it on, then grabs her purse and we head for the door. Mom is on the other side.

She looks at Stacey. "All done?"

Stacey leans in, kissing my cheek. "I'll be in touch."

Chapter 3

Michael

There has been no word on Jamie's whereabouts—no credit card information, not even her bank account has been touched. Every day everyone around me loses hope, but I refuse to believe she's gone. I refuse to let her go.

The police found the SUV off the road after slamming into an embankment and Josh was outside of the vehicle where he had been shot. With all the phone calls and the break in at the apartment, the police are thinking he did it all, but any hope for a break in the case ended with him.

I sit at the main bar in 42 for a couple of hours, going over every detail of that night. It feels like a knife sticking inside of me and it twists each passing day she's gone with no clear answers. Everyone tries to console me, or they avoid me. But this brown bottle of liquid on the bar is the only thing that keeps my mind off the never-ending ache in my body. Seeing the bottle is now empty, I raise my hand for another.

"Stuart, one more."

"Hey boss, how about some food or coffee?"

"No, I don't think so, but I can get it myself." I slide off the barstool when my arm is caught by someone. I look at who I'm about to punch. "Pete! Do you want a drink? I'm about to get another."

"Michael, you can't go behind the bar." He looks at Stuart. "Put an order in for a pot of coffee with a turkey sandwich and send it upstairs."

Stuart nods and walks away from us. Pete holds me firmly with both hands.

"You can let go."

"No, I can't. Let me help you. Jamie wouldn't want you to do this to yourself."

Just the mention of her name rushes around in my head, clouding all rational thinking. Pete understands my pain—she meant a lot to him. I just nod in agreement.

"I don't know what to do."

"We can do it together."

We enter the office which I've only sat in a few times since her disappearance. It's been the last thing on my mind.

"You don't quit. Michael, I know you miss her, and you're in hell right now, but this is not the way. You said you felt her around—do you still feel her?"

"I do."

"Whatever happened to her, you'll find out, but for now, you must stop blaming yourself and get back on track so you can continue the search. I can hold down the bar until you're ready, but I would like you back."

I place my hands over my face, then sit back on the sofa. "Nothing has ever hurt this much."

"That pain is what will keep you going."

Stuart brings in a tray and I stand, holding out my hand.

"Sorry about before."

"It's okay, we're all here for you. Jamie means a lot to us."

He shuts the door gently behind him when he leaves.

"Michael, trust in the love you have for her. Know that the day will come, and your pain will end."

"You miss her too."

"She's like a daughter to me. I pray for you both every day."

He leaves and I force myself to eat half the sandwich, then lie down on the sofa. This time when I fall asleep, I have hope.

*

I decide to take Pete's advice and get back into school, back to work, and taking care of myself. I start running again, using it as therapy like Jamie did. I pour all my free time into the extra shifts at work while preparing for graduation. My search for the real reason why Jamie was with Josh or why she left me is still unanswered, but never out of my mind.

I haven't told my parents about Stacey's pregnancy accusations, but I privately secure a lawyer and will have an ordered paternity test when the baby is born. I eat most days at the 42 and sometimes Pete's house. He knows me and is able to say all the things to keep me on track. As for my parents, my father has done a complete turn for the better. He helps whenever I ask and has agreed with me on not going to grad school. He calls regularly and shows up randomly sometimes without my mom, restoring my faith in us building a better relationship.

*

My parents are in town today for my graduation. I stand in front of the newly replaced bathroom mirror in my graduation gown, thinking back on the plans Jamie and I had before she went missing. It's been two months and I still feel her very close to me. I pick up the black box that holds the engagement ring I bought for her, placing it securely in my pocket. No one knew about my plan to propose.

My dad clears his throat as I walk out to my bedroom. "Today is the day."

"Yes. How do I look?"

"Like a college graduate." He pulls papers out of his coat pocket. "Before we go out there and your mother starts crying again, I want you to know how proud I am of you. I know we have struggled over the years and I take full responsibility for our relationship in the past, but I am actively working to keep us moving forward. I witnessed your suffering and I know you love her very much. I am proud of the man who stands before me. I love you."

I walk over to him, placing my arms around him. "I love you too Dad, but I take half of the responsibility of our relationship falling apart. I want to thank you for being supportive of me these past two months and not telling me I'm crazy. My fight for her will continue every day I have breath in me."

We both take a minute to collect ourselves, then he hands over the papers. "The 42 is all yours."

"I don't understand. We talked about me buying it upon graduation."

"Son, you love that bar and it shows in your employees and the great relationship you have with the college and community. I want you to have it."

I reach for the papers, flipping through them. "I don't know what to say."

"You and Pete will make it even better once you devise a plan of your own by implementing the changes you have always wanted. Maybe you can open new locations in other states."

My mother comes into the room. "Are you gentlemen ready?" Her tissue filled hand goes to her eyes, blotting away tears. "I'm so proud of you," she says, hugging me.

I look at them both, feeling as though our family is getting a new start. Touching my pocket where the ring sits, I hold out for the reality that one day she will be with us.

I smile at them both. "Let's graduate."

Chapter 4

One year later
Jamie

oming through the door of the gallery after my extended time away from work, I hear a familiar voice.

"Stop! Hold up! What are you doing?"

"Alysse, my sweet friend, you are the one who brought me all of these files to look over at home. I'm bringing them back to you sorted, labeled, and ready for filing."

"Really?"

"Yes."

"You were to look over them, not do them."

"Well you know me, not doing them wasn't an option."

She opens her arms taking the stack of files. "Welcome back boss, I've missed seeing your face around here."

"It feels good to be back in the swing of things."

A high-pitched squeal is heard behind us. "Jamie, I'm so glad you are back. You look good, love the new hair color."

"Thanks Tanner. I saw the web sales for your jewelry line last night, fabulous."

"Oh my God, it's better than I could have ever dreamed. I owe you big time for this job and for believing in my dream."

"It's all you, so get me more to put on the site."

"Yes, ma'am, I'm working on it."

*

I walk up the steps leading to my office, thinking of all the phone calls I need to make today. Inside my office, I find a big bouquet of flowers on my desk. "How pretty, who are they from?"

"The set-up crew. They're happy you're back and don't have to work with me and my crazy self any longer."

"I'll thank them later. Also, I like your crazy." I stand behind my desk looking at the stacks of new submissions as she proceeds.

"The callbacks are in order of importance along with a ton of emails since Friday. I weeded out all the junk."

"Good to know."

"Robert wants to see you as soon as possible and then there is the final walk through with Randall for his showing tonight."

"Oh, that's right, our new artist, Randall."

She sits casually on my desk. "You mean the father of my future children? The gorgeous artist who expresses himself through metal while sporting the most beautiful tattoos I have ever seen, Randall."

I giggle. "Someone is smitten?"

"Just a bit." She turns to leave.

I move the flowers onto a side table where I can enjoy them. Next a bathroom break, hot tea, and then off to find Robert.

While washing my hands, I take a deep breath, closing my eyes and then slowly exhale.

You can do this Jamie, you've been doing it for over a year.

I open my eyes and see my new lighter hair—just another way to hide myself. I tuck my blouse inside my grey skirt and open the bathroom door to step outside into the hall where I see my boss. Robert Shaw is a tall slim grey-haired gentleman in his early fifties and the proud owner of Shaw Galleries. Robert, along with his wife Savannah, took me in when I arrived in New York. They saved me and for that I will always be grateful.

"Jamie, I was coming to see you. How's your morning so far?"

"It was challenging to get out the door."

He touches my elbow. "I'm sure it was but immerse yourself into your work and the day will fly by. Are we all set for tonight?"

"Yes sir. Randall will be in later for the last walk through of the exhibit and with a few changes I want to make in two displays, we should be ready."

"I'm sure he will approve. We've missed you around here. This division of Shaw Galleries is made for you. I know talent when I see it." He starts to walk away, calling over his shoulder, "Let me know if you need anything. Savannah left you a surprise in your office for tonight. You're the daughter we never had, so spoiling you is what she loves to do. Now go make me lots of money."

"Yes sir."

*

After meeting the set-up crew downstairs and thanking them for the flowers, I head up to work in my office. After a few hours, my phone buzzes.

"Yes Alysse?"

"Jamie, Randall Scott is here to see you."

"Of course, send him in." I open the door just as he appears. "Good morning Randall."

"Jamie, it's good to see you. First day back, huh?"

"Yes, but all is good so far. How are you feeling?"

"Nervous. My first showing is either going to make me or destroy me."

I pour him a glass of water. "Look, you did the hard part by creating such beautiful pieces for us to show. We have the displays ready for your last walk through, some papers to sign like we discussed, then that's it. The rest is easy."

"I am very grateful for the opportunity, but I don't want to let you guys down."

"Not a chance. Tonight, you mingle, talk about your passion for metal and let us handle the rest. Do you have any questions?"

"No. You have more than accommodated my needs."

"Great. Let's head down to your exhibit."

*

After going over the final details on his showing Randall leaves, feeling pleased and a little less stressed. Alysse and I eat lunch, going over tonight's details, then I spend twenty minutes or so alone in my office when Tanner buzzes me.

"Yes?"

"Jamie, there is a gentleman down here to see you."

"A new artist?"

"No, I don't think so."

"Let him know I'll be right down." Slipping on my heels, I proceed down to meet whoever has stopped by today.

Tanner is smiling, almost giddy. "He's real hot."

"Well, let's keep that comment to ourselves, though now you have me a little curious. Did he ask for me specifically?"

"Yes. Should I go meet him with you?"

I smile at her. "No, I got this."

I enter the lounge to find a man dressed in khaki pants with a blue blazer looking over one of the pictures on the wall with his back to me. A leather satchel sits in one of the chairs with the initials, "MT."

With my eye still on the satchel I begin to speak. "Excuse me sir, I hope I haven't…"

He turns to face me as my hands cover my mouth and I struggle to breathe. I can't tell if this is real or every dream I have dreamt since leaving Hopson. My words are gone and so is my ability to stop the tears already filling my eyes. I can't believe what I'm seeing.

Michael Tucker is an arm's length away from me and when he says my name, I fall into the chair behind me, closing my eyes and not wanting to look up to find him gone. He approaches me, bending down and placing his hands on my knees, applying a firm pressure as he seems to reassure himself that I'm also real. His voice wavers.

"Jamie, look at me. I need you to look at me."

I blink away tears and open my eyes to look at his hands on mine. "Are you real?"

"I am."

He touches my face, wiping tears away as his own fall. My heart breaks all over again. I pull his head down onto my lap and bend so I can lay my cheek against his hair. He lets out a sound that I can only believe is relief. When he lifts his head, he looks into my eyes.

"I've thought about this day for so long. I never gave up hope that someday I would find you." He sits by me in another chair holding onto my hands as I hold onto his.

"Are you alone?" I look past him nervously. This is when I start to panic, fearing what he might say.

"Yes. I'm here on business. I had a meeting that was postponed up the street just a few blocks away from here, so I started walking and saw the name 'Jamie Carson' in the window."

"You saw my name?"

"Yes." He takes me to the window display. There is indeed a sign with my name on it for tonight's showing.

"I've never put my name in the window of a display," I say, somewhat bewildered.

"Well I need to thank the person who did. Without me seeing it, I would have kept walking. Jamie, I need to know what happened. You've been gone for over a year. Why didn't you contact me? What did I do?"

I turn away from the window wringing my hands as I always do when I get nervous. He notices right away, taking one of them in his.

"You did nothing. I left out of fear for your life, for the baby she was claiming to be yours."

"So, she did tell you."

"Yes."

He steps away from me, running his hands through his hair in frustration. "Did you believe her?"

"No, I didn't believe the baby was yours. You and I had already dealt with that night." I begin to panic. "Was she really pregnant?"

"Yes. She came to me. I went home from the hospital after the accident. She told me about the pregnancy. At that time, I didn't know if she had something to do with your disappearance so I played along. But I felt Caleb might be the father."

"Caleb?"

"Yes. So much so that with his consent I had papers drawn up and a paternity test was done right after the birth. Before the results were read, she disappeared, signing over her rights of the boy to him."

"A boy."

"His name is Eli. He's healthy and happy and Caleb has taken to fatherhood naturally, along with a fair amount of support from his family. I've been dubbed Uncle Michael." He looks at me. "Jamie, on that night, why were you with Josh?"

"I wasn't with him willingly. He took me from the apartment. I fought to get away but was knocked unconscious and taken to a warehouse. When I woke up, I was tied to a chair. Stacey was there with him."

"So, she did know him."

"Yes."

"Please, I need to know everything."

"Stacey told me that I'm her sister."

"What? That can't be true."

"She has the proof. I saw it."

"Did she break into the apartment? Maybe she's using that information."

"No...well yes. It was Josh. With the information he retrieved from me, she had the opportunity to start a search."

"This makes no sense. She never said she had a sister when we were together."

"After her mother's death, she found journals, a photo, even the baby blanket that matches the corner from my father's belongings. She found out her father was not her biological father; with her mother's passing, she was unable to get answers to any of her questions, so she devised a plan."

"Plan?"

"From what she said, I feel she had something to do with her father's unfortunate accident that left him unresponsive, giving her access to his business affairs. His family has money and she needed to control him to have power of attorney. She moved him to Italy and didn't tell them where he was, allowing her to handle his affairs. She changed her name so she couldn't be tracked, moved out of Texas, and came to Hopson because of you."

"Why me?"

"Your family's wealth matched with the control she now had would put her financially where she wanted to be. The only thing she didn't count on was you falling in love with me."

"I never lived in Texas. How did she find out about me?"

"An interview. You were on the news. Some interview that was done about your father's company that led to you being at Hopson. Michael, she said there were people she could call, and your parents would die in a freak accident, or she would terminate the pregnancy if you didn't accept her. I fought with Josh after your accident, which is why we ran into an embankment. It left us hurt, but he was coughing up blood. He began to tell me more of her plan."

"Why?"

"I think he knew he was going to die. He told me to run, leave town, and never contact you. It was the only way to keep you safe. He called her, told her I ran once the accident happened, and he never saw me."

"She bought that?"

"No. I took a few steps away from him to go to you, when he choked out the words 'It's her.' He told me to run into the woods and not to look back. I reached just inside the tree line when I heard a shot fired. I turned as the car was sitting beside Josh's SUV. I panicked because if she could do that, then killing others would be easy for her. I saw another car pull up near you and then heard sirens so I knew you would get the help you needed, and that's when I ran."

He takes me into his arms, holding my head to his chest and I turn, leaning my ear against him. I listen to the sound I'd longed to hear, the beat of his heart mixed with the warmth of his body. It makes my senses wake up. He smells of cologne, clean and woodsy. I wrap my arms around him as tight as I could and feel a long heavy weight leave my body. I feel free for the first time in over a year. He feels the release and kisses the top of my head.

"How can I ever take away all of the pain she has caused you?"

"I caused you pain, I stopped the life we would have had because I didn't know of any other way. I'm sorry for leaving without any word of what happened to me, but I feared for your life. Will you ever be able to forgive me?"

"I don't blame you. I never gave up hope that one day I would find you. It was that hope that made me crawl out of bed every day. It was the memory of you that has kept me going. I had Pete, my parents, and the guys to support me, but Jamie who did you have?"

I take his hand, putting it on my chest. "I had you right here along with every memory we created. And I also held onto hope that one day I would be back in these arms again."

He pulls away, moving a piece of my hair behind my ear and cups my cheek. Lowering his lips to mine, he stops.

"Wait, is there someone in your life that will kick my ass if I kiss you right now?"

"No, there has been no one." I roll up my sleeve showing him the bracelet with the word 'forever' he gave to me at Hopson. "I still believe in our forever."

His mouth lowers to mine. We connect like we always had before, melting our two universes together as one. After a year away from him, my body gives into feeling the rush that he causes. I'm weak not just from seeing him for the first time since leaving, but because of the power he has over me. He stops kissing me and looks past me, rubbing his finger across my cheek.

"We have an audience."

I turn to see my coworkers standing there, confused by what they've just encountered. I giggle, and he kisses me on my nose.

"Have dinner with me tonight."

"I would love to, but I have a showing here at eight. Do you want to come by? You'll need a suit."

He smiles. "I can manage that. Your receptionist told me this is your first day back, everything okay?"

"She says too much. Give me your phone." He hands it to me. "I'm sending a text from you to me with the address to the gallery."

"How do I leave you now that I've got you back?"

"I'm not running anymore."

His phone rings. Without taking an arm from around me, he answers it. "I'll be right there. Thank you."

"I'm late for the meeting." He grabs his satchel and continues to hold my hand as he walks towards the door, kissing me again. "I've missed you."

Those few words threaten another breakdown, but I pull him into a kiss. "I've missed you too. We have so much more to talk about."

"We do. I'll be back at eight."

*

Tanner touches me after he leaves. "What was that about?"

Alysse stands with her arms crossed. "That was Michael, wasn't it?"

"Yes."

"Are you okay? I mean how, why today?" Her arms go around me. "Jamie, what are you thinking right now?"

I shake my head trying not to cry. She hooks her arm in mine ushering me up the stairs.

"What are the odds that he would just walk into the gallery today?"

"There's a sign in the window with my name, and I want to thank whoever did it. He stopped because he saw it. I feel like my heart is going to explode."

"Why is he in town?"

"Work. I'll find out more later when he comes back. I invited him to the showing." My phone buzzes.

It's Michael in front of "Sampson's Bar" a few blocks down the street with the words *"my new project."*

I text back, *"Staying in town I hope?"*

He replies, *"Definitely."*

Alysse pulls out her phone. "I'll move your 4:00 meeting today so you can get out of here and prepare for tonight. I can't believe this is happening."

I look at my phone, then at her. "When I tell him everything, what if it's all too much?"

"It won't be."

Chapter 5

Jamie

I stand in the gallery ready to represent another young artist. My job is to advise, support, and sell the new, young, upcoming artist. Randall's job is to speak about his passion for metal. But I'm thinking about Michael—it's all I've done since seeing him earlier.

"Jamie. Jamie?"

"I'm sorry Robert. I'm a little preoccupied."

"I heard about earlier. Don't be mad—Alysse told me. You know since you arrived in New York, Savannah and I have taken you into our hearts, welcoming you into our family. If this young man is who you want, my only fear is how long before he takes you from us?"

"Both of you have done so much for me. It's just…"

"I see that you are worried about telling him everything, but don't be. Just give him time to process it all. You both went through a lot, more than most."

I give him a hug. "Thank you."

"Give me a sign if you need my help tonight." He winks, walking away.

*

After a quick trip upstairs to make a phone call, I come back down again to see Randall speaking with Alysse.

"Excuse me, but Randall what do you think?"

"I feel it's not me." He waves his hands. "I mean, how did I get to this point actually represented by a gallery?"

"You care about each one and it shows. You brought them to life. This is all you."

"I appreciate all you have done for me. You run a good program and care about us newbies. Alysse showed me the online bids for 'A Walk in The Park.'"

"That piece will bring so much more before the night is over. Relax, go get a drink. I'll catch up with you later."

Alysse winks at me and I watch my nervous artist head to the bar.

*

I turn to look if Michael has arrived when I see him next to Exhibit #4 dressed in a black suit. I'm nervous, checking over my dress and smoothing out the fabric as I make my way to him.

"I like your suit."

"Thank you. You look stunning." He leans over kissing my cheek.

I start fidgeting in my heels as my cheeks warm at the touch of his lips. Savannah had sent me a blue lace sheath dress for tonight. It fits beautifully accentuating my legs.

He takes my hand. "Are you blushing?"

"How about I give you a tour of the gallery? And yes, I am." We end the tour at the wine/beer station. "Would you like a drink?"

"Yes, thank you."

He's watching my every move. I ask the attendant for his favorite.

"You remember."

"I remember everything about you. It's what I had to keep me going."

He looks away, turning up his beer, then says words that crush me. "It hurt to think about you. Every day I woke up wishing you were with me. I lost myself a few times. I don't blame you leaving. I blame the monster who did this to us."

Curtis moves up beside us. "Jamie, we need your assistance."

I nod okay to him then look at Michael. "I have to go."

"I understand."

I walk away with Curtis but then stop, turning to Michael.

"I missed you every minute of every day we've been apart. You consumed my thoughts and took over my dreams. There is so much I need to tell you."

He captures my attention with a kiss. "I want it all."

*

He sends my mind into a frenzy, but I need to concentrate on the show and hold everything inside. After handling a computer problem with an online buyer, I walk out, looking for our artist.

Alysse is right by his side taking notes, which is a good sign that people are talking. Randall is busy with one of our regulars from "Shultz," a big advertising firm here in the city. She sees me and follows me to the desk.

"How is Mr. Hottie?"

I look over at Michael. "He's good, but I'm barely holding it together."

"Look, I won't let you fall into that dark hole again. He's right here, you're right here. You both have a second chance."

"I hope he understands."

"Are you going to tell him tonight?"

"Yes. I need to know everything about him, and he needs that from me."

"I do agree he needs to know, but tonight?"

"Yes."

She taps my arm with her elbow. "I see someone else is curious about him."

I look over at Michael to find Maggie McMillian as she smiles, flips her hair, then tucks her hand inside Michael's arm. She is one of Shaw Galleries' best buyers, so I guess I must play nice when what I really want to do is go over and rip her hand off his arm. But that would be a little aggressive.

"Jamie, wasn't she wearing that cobalt blue dress to the Holt Exhibit?"

"Yes, and she looks good in it."

"Are you jealous?"

"Damn right, but do I have that right?"

"Oh, you do. Look, her hand is on his back. She's quick to take claim."

We're brought out of our conversation by Robert who is straightening his tie, waiting for us.

"Jamie, are you ready to do the official introductions?"

"Yes sir, I am."

He clears his throat and gets the attention of the crowd. He introduces himself, then tells a little about the gallery, before introducing me. I begin with my name and title, why we are here, tell Randall's background story, then introduce him. He beams with pride when speaking about his art and I see he's now comfortable. Alysse hands me a tally sheet. I announce that in the last half hour, two of his pieces have sold with a big thank you to Palmer & Associates law firm and that they signed for two more pieces for their new location in Manhattan. He is over the top excited as everyone claps.

"Now are you at ease knowing this information?"

"It's cool, very cool. Thank you for all the long hours of keeping me on schedule. I will recommend Shaw Galleries to anyone wanting to get their foot in the door and their art into the public."

"Thank you for that. We will meet next week to discuss tonight's sales and where we go from here." I feel a tap on my shoulder. "Randall, this is Mrs. Franklin and she owns Little's Book Store, she has expressed interest in Exhibit 5, so I am going to let you two talk."

*

After tending to the online bids, I walk away to grab a glass of wine, taking a few sips to calm my own nerves.

"I missed your birthday. How much more did I miss?"

That would be a great intro to what I need to tell him, but instead I take another sip.

"Maybe coming tonight while you had to work was a bad idea. I'm just having a hard time being away from you since finding you this morning."

I hold out my hand. "Come with me."

I take him to the back of the gallery, setting my glass down on a table where we can have a little privacy.

"You're right, maybe inviting you to the showing was not a good choice. When you left the gallery earlier, I felt over-the-top excited, but scared at the same time."

"Why?"

"I fear you won't be able to forgive me for what I did or what I still need to tell you."

He backs me up against a pillar hiding us from the other guests touching my lips with his thumb, moving down to my collarbone. He looks at me touching my soul as only he can. I grab his coat to steady myself.

"I spent hours wondering why you were with Josh or what did I do for you to run without talking to me. The police kept telling me you were dead, that too much time had passed. But I fought against them. I was out of my mind, lost and lonely without you. I fell into drinking, didn't attend school or the bar. I was angry, pissed at everyone who didn't give me answers. Pete stepped in, guiding me to what I needed to do. My day to day life continued without you, but you were always with me. What you did for me, for my family, makes my love for you even stronger. You sacrificed, dealt with all of this by yourself, but I'm here for you now. Whatever you need to tell me will be okay. Nothing is tearing us apart ever again."

"How can you be so sure?"

He leans forward, barely brushing my lips with his, intensifying the feeling in my body, and kisses me. I whisper his name before leaping over the edge of no return. It's a deep kiss as we claim each other, not caring where we are. We stop kissing when an alert from my phone goes off.

"I need to get back. Will you be staying until the end of the show?"

"I'm not leaving until you do."

I pull him down to me for one more kiss. This time I smile, walking away from him a little drunk on the feelings he's stirred. I've waited for a miracle and today is proof they do exist.

*

When the last customer left, Curtis locks the doors as we all clap, cheering for Randall and his success tonight. He announces he wants us all to keep the party going over at Shine Bar. Before I agree, I look for Michael and find him in the lounge looking at the picture from earlier.

"There you are."

He turns and smiles at me. "All done?"

"Yes, but they want to celebrate at a bar near us called Shine."

"I'm in if you are."

"Good."

"Jamie, why do I feel I've seen this picture before?"

"You haven't actually seen it, but I've spoken about it many times. It's the field of flowers with the pond at my home in Texas."

"You painted this?"

"Yes."

"How did it come to hang here in the gallery?"

"I left Hopson with very little on me. When I decided to sell my truck, I had cash, which led me to the train station. I bought a ticket straight to New York. The city offered me a place to get lost. I was off the train for three days still looking for a job and staying at the Y when I saw a sign in their window. Shaw Galleries was running a two-week program to find young artists for an idea they had, which turned into the young artist division you saw parts of tonight. It was held here in the gallery. They produced all kinds of materials for us to use and it gave me an escape each night until ten to be somewhere else. I poured my feelings into several drawings and paintings. I didn't say much to anyone but on the fourth night a girl asked me for help. So, I helped her. Then I helped another girl with her jewelry creations."

"Tanner?"

"Yep. Robert noticed something in me that I thought was gone forever."

"Which was?"

"Life. I had nothing to give to anyone, but when I picked up the charcoals and paint, it helped me sort through things without telling anyone how I arrived here. Robert said he saw potential in my work. He and Savannah invited me to dinner and I was asked to be their first artist the gallery would represent for this program. I didn't have an apartment of my own, so I came and worked in the back room for a few weeks. I felt I would have been consumed by grief, if it had not been for the opportunity here at Shaw. I sold eight out of ten items the night of my showing. I received contracts from two local restaurants, one bookstore, and a children's doctor's office. That gave me the idea to enroll in night classes, but I couldn't get my transcripts from Hopson, so I started over. I filled every minute with reading, homework, or my art. Robert spoke to me about being the new representative of the young artist division, which I accepted.

"I'm happy you had people to help you. I owe them my gratitude. The painting is really beautiful."

"He said it reminded him of his childhood. Are you ready?"

He reaches for my hand. "Yes."

*

We decide to walk to Shine. I steal glances at him, not quite believing he's right beside me. My coworkers give me looks; I've never been with a man around them before. One day changes everything. I gently squeeze his hand.

"You will like Shine—it has good energy. The picture you sent me earlier…what kind of project is it?"

"When I graduated, my father gave me the 42. It's legally all mine. I now travel around looking for new locations for new bars. I first started traveling because I thought maybe I would see you walking on a sidewalk or drinking coffee at a café."

"Or find me while walking to a meeting?"

"Exactly. The bars all have signature drinks and 50% of the sale of those drinks go towards a cause or need in that area. I adopted your non-profit ways."

"You were the one who saved cardboard and cans to donate to the no kill dog shelter in college. The 42 fits you. Do you have a home office?"

"Yes, in my father's building. At each bar I have an office along with a manager that I depend on to run it when I am not there."

"It sounds wonderful. How many do you have?"

"I have the 42 in Hopson, Teagan's in Denver, and this new one here. My parents have been very supportive. You could say my dad and I have come full circle and our relationship is stronger than ever. They're also in a better place as a couple. She pitches in helping at the office and he helps her at home. When they're not taking little trips together, they enjoy their other hobby."

"Which is?"

"Each other."

My mouth flies open. "Oh, that's great."

"It is until you have to witness it." He bumps my shoulder shaking his head.

"Well I'm sure your mother feels better about that, but more about the two of you getting along."

"It's what she always wanted."

Our crowd stops in front of Shine. Randall speaks up.

"First round is on me, then we are all dancing in celebration of my sales and the wonderful staff at Shaw Galleries!"

Chapter 6

Jamie

hine is exactly what we both needed. The drinks, dancing, and stealing a couple of moments at a corner table help us to relax. In the cab, I give the driver my address only to see Michael smile at me.

"Is that okay that we go back to my apartment?"

"Yes."

"Why are you smiling?"

"I just have fond memories of a particular cab ride home the night of the ECON fundraiser."

"I remember it well."

He reaches for my hand tucking it in his.

We arrive in front of my building which is an old warehouse turned into loft apartments. The windows are huge, running all the way across the front. Michael pays the driver, then stands on the sidewalk looking at the brick building.

"This is impressive. Look at all the details. What was it before?"

"A shoe factory. Lots of old wood floors, and storage. I share my space with art pieces from the gallery. Let's go up."

We pass through the entrance which is outfitted with industrial looking furniture forming a sitting area, mailboxes, and a little corner of the room with the history of the building. The elevator is empty except for us. I'm nervous again as I rock my foot back and forth waiting for my floor as the buzzer goes off.

The elevator stops.

"This is me." I dart out of the elevator over to my door trying to fit the key into the lock as his hand covers mine.

"Let me help you." He takes the key, gliding it in on the first try. "Jamie what's wrong?"

"Let's go inside so we can talk."

My door opens to an entrance lined with two wooden benches and lots of different hooks on the walls. He helps me out of my coat, hanging it up. I begin to rattle off details of the apartment, then ask him if he wants water or coffee. We walk further inside and he glances around the loft.

"Michael, I need to talk to you."

He bends down behind the sofa bringing something up with him.

"What's this?"

"A burp cloth. I have a roommate."

He lays it on the back of the sofa and notices a baby swing. "Your roommate has a baby?"

"The baby is my roommate." That sounds stupid, so I blurt it out. "The baby is mine."

The look on his face is crushing. His brow wrinkles and his eyes continue to scan the room, before his attention lands on me.

"You said you hadn't been with anyone. I don't understand."

"The baby is yours."

I did it. If words could be seen, those four just hit him in the face and broke into a thousand pieces.

He turns away and walks to the window, running his hands through his hair. I sit on the coffee table and pick up a soft rattle. He stands with his hands on the sill. His silence makes me want to jump out of my skin as I wait for him to respond.

"We have a baby?"

"Yes."

"Boy or girl?"

"Boy. He's twelve weeks old. I just got back from maternity leave."

"Where is he now?"

"Next door with Ruby."

"Ruby knows about the baby? She knows about today?"

"Yes. The phone calls I got tonight were from her. She was the one who suggested she keep him tonight, so we could talk."

He spots photos on the table next to him, picking up one. "What is his name?"

"Benjamin Michael Tucker, I call him Ben."

He walks over to the sofa in front of me and sits. "What's he like?"

"He's healthy with dark eyes, brown fuzzy hair, and round, squeezable cheeks."

I can't stand the look on his face. He's looking at Ben's picture and I don't know what he's feeling. I go to stand up when he reaches for my wrist.

"Stay. I want to know about him."

I sit back down. "He was born on Wednesday, December 28 at 2:35 am. He was 21 inches long and weighed 8 lbs. 7 oz."

"Was it hard going through it alone?"

I swallow as tears began to fall down my cheeks thinking back to the way I felt, and the hopeless feeling of not being able to share this amazing gift we had been given.

"Keeping him from you almost killed me, but I knew if I told you she could find out."

"I should have been with you."

"Yes, you should have been with me, but I couldn't. I worked my job, kept my doctor's appointments and ate the right kind of food to keep him healthy. I survived the days knowing he was inside of me, but every night I went home alone I slipped into darkness. I had cut ties from Ruby, from Susan, from anyone that Stacey could know and possibly find out about the pregnancy. In my mind, knowing what she was capable of gave me no room for error. As months went by the fear that gripped me just seeing someone on the street that resembled her, swept me further away from going out, running, or even attending public functions at work. Savannah asked me one day if I had family? When she said that, I began to cry. I told her I did, but I was unable to be with them. A week later I got sick, had a fever that weekend, and began to talk in my sleep. She said I mentioned the name Michael and that at one point I started crying. I spoke about Ruby and how I missed her. I was so careful not to let anyone from here into my world, but she acted like any mother would and searched my apartment. She found journals I had written in since arriving in New York. She found Ruby, then had her cousin who lived in Texas call her. Ruby was here the next day."

"How did she take the news you were..."

"Alive. It was difficult for her not knowing what happened to me like it was for everyone. She told me you talked with her. I got quite the talking to once I was feeling better. She understood my need to keep you safe because she knew how much I loved you. She wanted me to contact you, but I couldn't. She said you would keep us all safe, but I just couldn't chance it. Her being here gave me the strength to fight for the one part of you I had. I told him about you every day. I held your picture in front of my belly every night before I went to bed. I promised him that one day he would know you. Michael, I know you would have tried everything in your power to protect me, to protect our baby, but what she did to Josh was cold, brutal. She would not have hesitated at that point to do the same to me or to anyone I loved."

He rubs his face with his hands, moving closer to me and holding my knees between his legs. His eyes now have tears, feeling the pain of our time lost, his time lost with his son.

"I am so sorry I had to do this to you," I say.

"No, never be sorry for trying to protect the ones you love. You knew what she did, you knew she would not stop until she got what she wanted. I am glad Ruby was here for you if I could not be."

I take him into my arms as he took me into his. Nothing is ever going to erase for either of us what we endured apart, but now that it's out in the open, we can change from this day forward.

"You were not a part of his beginning, but you're here now. You found me today because we are meant to have the future we talked about."

He cups my face with his hands. "Promise me from this point on we face our future, no matter where it takes us, together. I will protect you and our son. No more tears or broken hearts."

"Agreed." I can't wait to tell you everything about him."

"What about Susan, does she know?"

"Ruby called her two weeks before I was due. She was here immediately."

He holds my hands, just taking in what I've told him, then glances up. "I'm a father."

"You are."

"I want it all. Spare me no details. What does he eat, what's his favorite toy, how do I change a diaper?"

I stand up. "Let me change out of this dress, then we can start from the beginning. Help yourself to anything in the kitchen. I'll be down the hall."

*

Michael

Jamie has gone to change her clothes and I loosen my tie, heading to the fridge to get us both some water. The counter holds bottles, nipples, and a few toys. I pick one up, then set it back down gripping my bottle of water.

I'm a father, I'm a father!

I go in search of her. She's standing at the foot of her bed struggling with the zipper on her dress.

"Let me help." She glances over her shoulder. I pull the zipper down slowly as my fingers brush against her skin, then lean in, laying a kiss on her exposed shoulder. Her skin smells of flowers, soft under my fingers. The fabric begins to fall off her when she catches it spinning to face me.

"I might look different. Pregnancy changes a woman's body."

I pull her in, tucking my hands behind her and kissing the wrinkles of her frown. "Let me see you."

She steps out of my arms dropping the dress to the floor. My eyes take in every inch of her. Head to toe she is beautiful. My eyes notice the fullness she is covering with her hands.

"I breastfeed." She looks down at the bra she is spilling over. "This is the first time wearing a pretty bra since delivery. It's a little small."

She's blushing, still covering her chest. I reach for her hands, taking them in mine.

"Impressive." She blushes more.

I push her gently back to fall on the bed as I remove my shirt. She props up on one arm gazing up at me.

"I have also changed."

She starts to giggle. "Yes, you too are bigger."

I drop on the bed beside her. "I was in the gym every day. I ran using that time as therapy like you always said you did, and it helped."

She smiles up at me with such sweetness. Her finger traces a scar on my neck.

"Is this from your accident?"

I take her finger to my lips, kissing it then her palm. "Yes."

She raises up placing a kiss on my scar, then moving to another. "I would take them all away if I could."

She places her hand against mine. At the same time, we both say, "They fit perfectly." She pulls me closer, kissing me, making me realize that we are about to make love for the first time in over a year when I stop.

"What's wrong?" Her fingers are in my hair, her eyes a deeper green full of lust just for me, but I have to ask.

"Are you okay to do this?"

Her left eyebrow raises as she smirks at me. "Oh yeah."

Jamie

With every kiss, or touch of his fingers on my skin I give in, wanting this moment to last an eternity. I've missed the weight of his body on mine along with the need to feel him. We claimed each other not leaving any inch of our bodies untouched. We began to release the pain, loneliness and guilt of the past year. Bringing each other back to life.

We lie in the bed, wrapped up in each with his fingers running a line up over my hip. He is home. My stomach on the other hand, lets us know the sweetness of our time is over as it summons me for food. He laughs.

"Hungry?"

"How did you know?" I pop up out of bed looking for something to put on when he meets me with his shirt.

"Would you? I've missed you wearing my shirts." He grabs me. "But I've missed you more out of my shirts."

He slips it on me, buttoning only two buttons.

"That's all?"

"Yes."

I take his hand pulling him with me to the kitchen and set out peanut butter and jelly as he unties the bread.

"I told Ruby we could get Ben about 7:30 in the morning if that's alright?"

"Yes, of course."

"Let's take this to the living room. I have something for you."

We begin to eat our sandwiches and after a few bites I get up and retrieve a photo album.

"From the time I found out I was pregnant this book began to tell our son's story. I wanted you to be able to relive his beginning."

He begins to flip through the pages of written entries as well as pictures of me pregnant and of his son. He stops at one entry, December 24th.

Today, my sweet little baby I share with you Christmas Eve. I have to say I am feeling sad because last year I was with your father. We attempted to make Ruby's famous yeast rolls but ended up in a flour battle. Your father is an amazing man. Have I ever told you how strong he is? Yep, inside and out. One day you could be like him. Oh, and this shirt that I am wearing is his. Just a little secret between you and me, I haven't washed it since leaving Hopson because it smells like him. The scent is faint as the days go by, but it's my favorite piece of clothing. It makes me feel closer to him. I promise you little buddy, that one day you will meet him, he will know you, and then you will know how incredible he is. Tonight, as I wrap my arms around my belly to hug you goodnight, I do it for your father as well. I love you so much.

"I knew you took the monogramed shirt and my grey hoodie. It gave me peace knowing you had it. In a way, I told myself you took it because you still loved me and wanted a part of me with you."

I crawl into his lap. "I took it along with the Colorado picture."

"The day I opened my door to you I needed to know everything about you."

"I remember that day. You made me feel like I was home."

"I'm glad you trusted me."

"I spilled so much to you the first night."

He notices Ben's hospital bracelet. "Do you know when he was conceived?"

"The night of the fundraiser. It was a big night filled with a creative cab ride home, a broken lamp, and some honey."

"You were angelic that night looking delicious covered in the golden sweetness. That was our last night together." He looks down rubbing my thighs with his thumbs. "If I had known you would be gone the next day, I never would have let you out of my bed that morning. We need to make some calls to let the police chief in Hopson know that you are alive."

I start to shake my head while moving off his lap, but he takes hold of my hands pulling me back down.

"Jamie, we can't hide any more. We lost each other once, I won't let that happen again."

"It may take some time for me to get there. To have your confidence."

"I know. But we will get there together."

I stand up reaching for his hand. "Let's grab a shower, so you can meet your son."

*

After our shower he goes to put on the shirt from last night, but I hand him another.

"You washed it?"

"Funny story. I was wearing it sitting over in that chair when my water broke. The shirt was soaked, and the cushion of the chair has been replaced. You can have it back."

"You don't want it anymore?"

"No because now I have the real deal." I hear the doorbell. "You ready?"

"I am."

Chapter 7

I open the door to see Ruby with Ben in the stroller. She sees Michael and goes to him immediately as I tend to our son. She's smiling, holding out her arms and loving that this moment is finally here.

"I'm so glad you are here. She loves you, you know that right?"

"I do. Nice to meet you in person Ruby, and I want to thank you for being here for Jamie."

"She's my girl. I did what I could, but she needed you."

"I understand."

"Look at me, I'm keeping you from your son. He is a precious baby. Jamie, call me if you need anything."

She kisses my cheek, leaving us alone. I hold Ben and walk over to Michael.

"Ben, I want you to meet your father."

Michael looks at him for the first time. He clears his throat, smiling through wet eyes. I can tell he is in love immediately. I touch his arm as he leans in to kiss me.

"Want to hold him?"

"Sure, what do I do?"

"Hold your arms like mine and support his head. He will wiggle." I hand him the baby capturing the moment forever in my mind. This is what I've wanted, what I dreamed about even before his birth. My tears are happy ones as Michael speaks to him softly. He looks at me.

"He is amazing."

"He is. Let's go sit on the sofa."

He moves Ben, placing him on his lap and cradling his head.

"I can't believe he belongs to us. We made him."

"We did. He is going to crush hearts someday. He already has mine."

"He has to share yours with me. I just met him, and I have an insane amount of love for him."

"Now you know why it's been so hard. He was the most important part of us. I couldn't take chances with him."

"I do understand. He is beautiful, but smelly."

"Want to change a diaper?"

His expression is unsure, but he stands up with Ben and follows me to Ben's room where his first diaper lesson takes place.

Next is a bottle. With a few instructions, I leave my two guys in the living room to bond and make a phone call to Alysse to take the day off. My family is all together now, and this is where I need to be.

Heading out into the living room, I see Michael has him over by the window.

"How did he eat?"

"Just like you said, and I burped him."

"High five daddy." He looks so surprised to hear me say it.

"I'm staying home today; do you have to go out?"

"Nothing is tearing me away from you guys today."

I reach over playing with our baby's feet. "Ben, we're playing hooky today."

"Look, he recognizes you."

"Your voice will be just as familiar to him, you'll see."

He smiles at Ben then hands me the baby. I walk to the sofa sitting down with him. "Feel like watching some videos?"

"If it has you and Ben in them, yes."

"I hope you feel the same about me after you see the birthing one."

"Hmm, that's the one I'm most curious about."

"I hope it won't scare you off. I mean—there are some pretty graphic shots. Susan held back nothing."

"Now I'm really interested."

Michael sits next to me with his eyes on Ben.

"Stay here with us. I don't know how long you'll be in town, but I want you here."

The look on his face is one of peace. "I would love to be here. Thank you. After lunch I'll close out my hotel room and call my office."

"Good. Here, you hold Ben and I will go get the DVD's."

*

It's after 4:00 in the afternoon and Michael is still gone. Ben is in his swing and I'm listening to music while folding laundry. He called a couple of hours ago and said he was running an errand and would be here right after. My doorbell rings and to my delight it's him, holding the handle of a red wagon.

"What's this?"

"I wanted to give him something, so I got him my favorite toy as a child. It will carry all of his most valuable possessions." He pulls it inside where I see a duffel bag, a brown grocery bag, and flowers. He scoops me up, kissing my neck. "Hello, gorgeous."

"I've missed hearing you say that."

He kisses me again, this time on the lips, leaving me to tingle all over.

"My plan is not to leave for a long time. Are you okay with me staying here for an undetermined length of time?"

"More than okay. I was going to give Ben a bath, do you want to help?"

"Yes, then I want to fix dinner for us. I also bought dessert along with a surprise for you."

"Me?"

"Yes. And, no I won't tell you what it is. But I will tell you we are having spaghetti."

"Yummy. Let's get you settled."

*

I leave the two of them to play in Ben's tiny tub while I retrieve some lotion. I'm getting hungry for the promised spaghetti and excited to see his duffel bag in my room. I join them in the bathroom.

"Don't you boys look cute?"

"He's not crying so I think all is good."

"Are you all done?"

"Yes."

I take Ben to dry him off, as Michael dries himself off.

"You might need another shirt." Before I finish that comment, he's pulled off the shirt, revealing a well-defined muscular frame. I smile over my shoulder. "Or no shirt works for me."

He begins to unbutton his pants. "How about no pants? You game?"

How I want to take him up on the no clothes game, but Ben is voicing his opinion about wanting dinner. I let out a sigh, still eyeing him.

"I guess we have to wait for adult play."

The fire in his eyes lets me know he's eager for the same play time.

I have fond memories of Michael's spaghetti dinners because it's the one dish he makes that is all his own and delicious every time. I enter the kitchen to see him standing barefoot in jeans wearing a tan t-shirt which strains against his broad shoulders and arms. I walk up and place my nose on his shirt, taking in his scent.

"Do you need help?"

"No." He turns, kissing my cheek. "I want to do this for you, so just relax."

"Sounds good. I'll just sit back here and look at you."

He grabs a towel to wipe his hands. "I need to tell you something. I hope you'll be okay with it."

"Sure, what?"

"I called my parents today."

Did he say he called his parents? I grab my glass of water, draining all the liquid. I fear what they might think of me leaving so abruptly, hurting their son like I did. I set down the glass, then bend over, putting my head between my legs.

He's right there in front of me, rubbing my back, then coaxes me up to face him. "It will be fine."

"I hurt their son. It won't be okay."

"It is. They're coming to New York."

I walk past him and refill my glass with water, then throw it back just like before. I turn my attention back to him.

"Do they hate me?"

"No. They're relieved you are safe and now with me. My mom is over the top about being a grandma."

"And your dad?"

"He's the one who wanted to come, ASAP. They don't blame you for leaving, Jamie. But I wasn't thinking. Maybe it's too soon."

I rest my hands on my hips. "There are a lot of people who may be furious with me, but I want Ben to know his family. The sooner the better." I walk over to kiss him.

*

After eating dinner, we put Ben to bed and take coffee and dessert to the living room. He sits down next to me.

"How was the spaghetti?"

"Delicious. You know how to spoil a girl, and now this beautiful plate of brownies."

"Before we eat those, I need to say something."

He reaches over taking my hand. The look on his face is serious.

"Is something wrong?"

"Jamie, I want to be the only man you will ever need for the rest of your life. I want to share birthdays, holidays, and every day through life's ups and downs."

He gets down on one knee in front of me.

"Michael, what are you doing?"

"I love you, I always have loved you. Will you marry me?" He opens a small black box which holds an amazing diamond ring.

"It's beautiful. Are you sure?"

"I've never been more sure in my life."

"Yes, yes, I will marry you!"

He pulls me up in a kiss and takes out the ring, sliding it on my finger.

"I was going to propose to you the day of graduation when we left for our beach trip. It's been in my pocket every day since, which is why the box is kind of worn out."

I slide my arms around his neck pulling him onto the sofa and tug on his beard.

"I love you so much. Thank you for not giving up on me."

"Not a chance."

I hold up my hand admiring my ring. "Mr. & Mrs. Tucker...I like the way that sounds."

Chapter 8

Jamie

S tanding in my closet wearing heels and a slip, I stare at my ring. I can't believe this is happening to us. My heart feels full for the first time in a long time. Two hands slide around my waist resting on my belly. I lean against him.

"Good morning. How did my fiancé sleep?"

"After our celebration of our engagement, very well. Do you like it?"

"I love my ring. But sir, you have only known me for a few days, are sure you want to marry me?"

"Time means nothing when it's real love."

"This is true. Are you sure you have to go in today?"

"Yes, Randall has had a ton of interest and I need to see him through the process."

We hear Ben on the monitor.

"I'll get him," Michael says and leaves as I pull on my dress.

"Are you sure you want to keep him by yourself today?" I call after him. "I'm sure Ruby could help."

He comes back in with our baby in his arms. "Ben, tell Momma we'll be fine."

"That's not it."

"I know. When I left yesterday, I stood outside the door, not wanting to leave you guys. Being present for this little guy and for you is important."

"Call me. Or I'll call you. Not to check up on you but to hear your voice because I don't ever want to stop hearing it."

*

Arriving at work today is so different from two days ago. I see Alysse in the exhibit area as I pass by.

"Good morning, Alysse."

She turns to me, putting her hand on one hip and raising her eyebrow.

"Why are you here and where's Mr. Sexy?"

"He's home with Ben. He's so cute with him. He's a big guy with a gentleness that makes my heart swell. He smiles constantly and talks in such a sweet voice to him."

"Well if you're trying to hide any of this happiness, it's hopeless." She grabs me in a hug. "I am so happy for you."

"I keep touching him to make sure he's real."

She hooks her arm through mine, fitting our hands together when she notices my ring and lets out the loudest scream.

"What is this? Did he propose to you? Tell me, tell me now!"

My lips can't stretch any further. "Yes, he did."

This time the hug is full of energy and extreme happiness.

"This is such good news, are you over the top?"

"I am. We want to do it as soon as possible."

"Well, let the planning begin. We're going to have a wedding!"

"We can talk it over at lunch, but right now we have a busy calendar today."

"Yes, we do."

*

Randall comes in to go over his incoming orders and afterwards, leaves to get started on the contracted pieces. Now it's straight paperwork for me, with more calls. A few hours have gone by and I need to stretch and take a quick walk out onto the platform above the gallery. But my eyes are diverted to Michael coming up the stairs.

"Is everything alright? Where's Ben?"

"Yes, and he's with Ruby. Can we talk?"

"Sure, come into my office."

I shut the door behind us when he gives me a delicious kiss. "I missed you the minute you left this morning."

"I missed you too. What's going on?"

"Last night we talked about my parents coming into town...well, it seems they're arriving in the next hour."

"That's good. Are you heading to the airport now?"

"I am. Can you go with me?"

"I wish I could, but my next meeting is in 20 minutes."

"Are you okay if they come to the apartment to meet Ben?"

"Michael, he is your son, their grandson. Of course I'm okay with it."

"I spoke to them about our precautions. Ben comes first and they agree."

"Thank you."

With another kiss he leaves to pick them up. I close my door taking in a deep breath or five to calm my nerves.

*

At five o'clock I start packing up to go home. In the car on the way to the apartment I start running all the possible scenarios of seeing his parents through my mind. He says they're different, but his father didn't think much of me before, so what's he going to think now? I received a text about an hour ago that stated his parents were in love with Ben, but that doesn't mean they have to be okay with me.

Leaving the elevator, I walk to the door and put in my key. I enter quietly, but the first thing I hear is laughter.

"There she is." Michael comes over to me, kissing me hello and searching my face for my current condition. I smile at him and think my eyes are about to pop out of my head.

"How's it going?"

"It's good. Come on over."

I see Mrs. Tucker holding Ben while Mr. Tucker sits next to her holding a soft toy. She stands with Ben and hands him to Michael as she steps towards me. She's always been very sweet, but I can't read what's about to happen. Her eyes have tears in them and she holds out her arms, embracing me in a hug.

"I'm so happy to see you," she whispers. "I'm sorry you both had to endure this past year apart. I never questioned your love for him and what you've done shows me how deeply you care. His eyes now have a spark of life that's been missing."

I shake my head. "I'm sorry I hurt him."

"You don't need to apologize. You were hurting just as much having to leave, but you both have a new life, with a new reason to keep fighting."

I wipe off my face. "They mean everything to me."

"I know they do. Ben is beautiful, a darling baby."

Mr. Tucker has also stood up and is next to Michael with his hand around his shoulders. I look at him.

"Mr. Tucker, it's nice to see you."

He walks to me. "It's good to see you, Jamie. Michael struggled, held onto hope, and showed me what real love is." He hugs me. "Welcome to the family."

Michael interrupts. "I told them we're engaged."

I wipe off my chin, smiling at his enthusiasm to share our news. Ben starts to fuss and I walk over to Michael, kissing our son.

"Yes, we are, and I am very happy, but I think Ben needs to eat. If you would excuse me, I'm going to take him into the bedroom."

Michael follows me down the hall with the baby and I sneak a peek back at them. His parents are in an embrace—a side I've never seen.

He looks at them. "Yep, they've been that way for a while. Kind of weird to watch."

I giggle. "Stop, it's sweet."

I wash my hands, then return to sit in the chair, coming out of my dress to feed Ben. Michael hands him to me, sitting across from us.

"Do you feel better about seeing them now?"

I look down at my sweet baby's face. "I do."

"Did you call Susan or tell Ruby yet?"

"I called Susan, but she was in class and I'll call later tonight. I wanted to tell Ruby in person."

"I spoke to Dad about my decision to move my home office here."

"Well, I was thinking about it. Why don't we make a home office in the apartment? Can we survive a little remodel?"

He comes over to me kissing my shoulder. "There isn't anything we can't get through, I think we proved that."

"We did."

Chapter 9

Jamie

It's been four days since meeting with Michael's parents, which was amazing. To witness Mr. Tucker with his grandson talking, smiling, and even feeding him a bottle is a huge change from how he was before. Business is now second to his wife and I love seeing the affection between the two of them even though Michael gets weirded out by it.

Our son had me up this morning at 4:30 fussing in his room. I kissed Michael on the shoulder, letting him know I was going to feed the baby and he could keep sleeping. After a fresh diaper, feeding, and another diaper my little man was still not sleepy, so we talked over plans for his mom and dad's new office. I even added to the list, through his suggestion, a play area made especially for him. After lots of cuddles he was back in his bed. I fixed a cup of tea and made my way back to the bedroom where Michael was still asleep.

I sip my tea, watching him stretched out on his back with the sheet resting just below his waist and clinging to his legs. He has one arm across his belly and the other one under his head. He stirs so many feelings in me all at once and I love it. It's now 6:15—time to wake him up, but how? I devise a plan as a couple more sips warm the inside of my mouth.

I set my cup on the dresser, then walk to the end of the bed. My hands are now on his ankles and I barely move the sheet, crawling my way onto the bed. I continue my cat like crawl up past his knees settling my hands on his thighs. He moves a little, but not quite enough for my liking. He takes in a breath, letting it out and I watch the breath leave through his parted lips. I smile to myself. Is he awake, letting me continue to tease him or asleep? I continue up to where the sheet rests, pulling it down and kissing right below his navel. I kiss his stomach, running my tongue across his skin. His body stretches, releasing a moan. He must be awake and playing with me. Well, let's see. I pull off my gown, then release my hair from its nest. I lean down, letting it touch him while I move up to his neck, leaving a couple of kisses and then gently pull at his lip with my teeth. His hand comes up to my neck pulling me into a deep, sexy kiss.

"Morning, gorgeous."

"I'm your alarm today."

"You're so much better than my phone."

He flips me so I'm now under him, nibbling down my neck onto my chest. I can feel his hands moving across my skin, teasing me.

"You're right, so much better than an alarm. Were you already awake?"

He gives me a fake attempt at a smile, then gives in. "I think you know the answer."

"I couldn't help myself. Your tanned skin under these white sheets makes it hard for me to resist you."

"Hmm, I think we're both going to be late for work."

*

His parents stay in town for two weeks to spoil their new grandson, but now they're back home missing him already. Today, Ruby has him all to herself. Michael has been working out issues with the new bar while meeting with distributors, contractors, and the city for permits. I signed three new artists with two shows happening this week. We've adjusted to our new life not taking anything for granted.

Our little family comes first so when the weather is good, we head outside. Today we're walking through the park with Ben asleep in his stroller while we enjoy a day in April without rain.

"You know soon he'll be playing in this park, running from us while getting into everything."

Michael reaches down and pulls the blanket up over Ben. "If he takes after me, getting into mischief will come natural to him."

"I hope he's just like you. It'll be fun."

The trees gently sway and the flowers are beginning to pop up with colorful blooms.

"Jamie, I don't want to wait." Michael has stopped and is looking at me.

"Wait for what?" I stop too.

"To marry you."

"We can get married anytime, all we need is a license." I start walking again, but he hasn't moved with the stroller.

"Haven't you thought about it?"

"A wedding? We don't really have many to attend and city hall will be fine, maybe dinner after."

"We should have a wedding."

I walk back to him. "I have been thinking about it. You really want to know?"

"Yes."

I tuck my arm in his and begin to walk. "A dress for me, you in a tuxedo, fresh flowers in soft pinks and white. Twinkling lights like the stars, a nighttime wedding. Oh, and a cake, vanilla pound cake."

"What about food?"

"Stick to your ribs food, no frilly small finger sandwiches unless they are sliders. If we do it in the city, a rooftop venue might be nice."

"You have been thinking about it."

"I have a sketch or two, yes of course I have, but I can also do city hall. What about you, what do you want?"

"I like the food idea, hearty choices. Cake, an open bar, and you and I ending the night as husband and wife."

"We'll get married soon, but I'm enjoying our engagement, being a fiancée."

He leans in, kissing me. "Me too."

*

Saturday night comes around and we're going out tonight with some friends to Shine. I stop at the dresser grabbing a bracelet when I hear a whistle.

"Thanks babe."

"Sexy is not a strong enough word to describe how you look right now. Maybe I should get you a coat."

"No way." I grab my purse. "Tonight, we party like rock stars because I've lost the last four pounds of baby weight!"

"Well then let's have this." From behind him he brings out two glasses. "Bourbon, interested?"

"So, we're on the same page tonight?"

"Yep. Ruby has Ben for tonight and I have you, so drink up woman."

*

Shine is one of the best places for dancing in the city. Michael gets out of the car, turning to me and holding out his hand to help me out. My dress falls to the side as I get out, revealing a lot of bare skin. A couple of guys passing by whistle. Michael shoots them a look to keep moving which makes me giggle.

"This momma still has it!"

"That you do." He kisses my hand, pulling me close.

The bar's inside matches our enthusiasm to cut loose tonight. Lights, people, and music only pump up my already elevated mood. He whispers in my ear that he is getting us drinks, then catches it between his lips, sending goosebumps down my arm.

"Don't be long." He walks away with a little grin. I spot Alysse coming towards me.

"You made it! Where is Michael?"

I point over at the bar. "He plans to get us drunk tonight." I smile my approval. "Oh, and I think my wedding sketches are going to be a reality soon."

"He can't wait, can he?"

"No. I told him city hall was fine."

"We can do better than that. We'll start planning Monday."

Michael walks up to us with drinks. "Ladies, the night has just begun, drink up."

We look at each other, then back at him, throwing back our shots. The song changes, and we drag him out onto the dance floor. After a couple of songs Randall shows up with some of his friends. Alysse goes over to greet him leaving us alone on the floor. Michael's hands grab my waist turning me, so my back is against him. We sync our movements.

"It's really hard for me to not touch you."

"So, I picked a good dress for tonight."

"Absolutely."

I flip around, running my hands up the front of his shirt, and wrapping them around his neck, bringing one down to rest on the buttons. I look up at him as my mind is suddenly flooded by the alcohol I've had tonight.

"Whoa, that was fast."

I giggle while pulling his lips onto mine. I kiss him, like I could devour him in one delicious bite. He smells so manly, stirring those butterflies inside my belly. He breaks our kiss resting his head on mine.

"Jamie, we're about to make a scene."

"Love makes us do funny things sometimes."

"Like getting us kicked out of here?"

"What can I say my love…you are irresistible? I know we haven't been here that long, but what do you say we go home?"

"Are you sure? You were looking forward to tonight?"

"I'm still looking forward to tonight, but at home. I'm going to the bathroom so when I return, we can go."

"Will you be okay while I grab two bottles of water?"

"Yes." I give him a kiss and leave in search of the bathroom.

On my way to the bathroom a tall blonde catches my eye. She's with a man who is holding her, kissing her next to a wall. I blink my eyes a couple of times to see her better. She starts kissing him on his neck, wrapping her arms around him and he spins her around so I can only see the side of her face. She flips her hair and that's when the hair stands up on my arms and a chill moves over me. I take a couple steps towards them, drawn to a need to know. Is it her? She turns her back to him as he grips her hips and she begins to move next to him. When she looks up her eyes land on me. It's not Stacey. I head to the bathroom trying to regulate my breathing, so I don't pass out. I take a few sips of water, splashing some on my cheeks.

It's not her, it's the alcohol making you freak out. Breathe, Jamie, just breathe.

Once I'm calmer, I use the bathroom, and wash my hands, looking at myself in the mirror again. There's a buzz of women around me, laughing but I'm falling once again back into the horror of that night. I feel a hand on my back and realize Alysse is speaking to me.

"Jamie, are you okay? Michael sent me in to check on you. He said you might be sick?"

"Alysse, we're going to leave."

"Let me get you some water—you're so pale."

"No, I just need to go home."

"How about I walk out with you?"

I nod in agreement. Outside the bathroom I see Michael with a look of concern on his face. I turn my attention to the woman on the dance floor, then back to him. He looks and it hits him.

"Jamie."

I'm trembling and it's all because I thought it was her. He pulls me in to his arms, resting his chin on my head. "Alysse, Randall's looking for you."

"Jamie, call me tomorrow."

I let go of him to hug her. "I thought I saw Stacey." I point to the woman on the dance floor. Alysse looks back at me, then at Michael, tightening her hug.

"I'm sorry, I've ruined our good time tonight."

"You haven't." She kisses my cheek. "I love you."

"Love you too."

I turn back to Michael. "Will this ever stop?"

He puts his arm around me and we leave Shine. The car ride home is quiet for us. He holds on to me as I try and shake off this bad feeling. We arrive at the apartment about 11:30. I want to call and check on Ben but deep down I know he's sound asleep and so is Ruby. I take off my shoes by the sofa, then collapse, sinking in the cushions. Michael has locked up, turned off the lights, and turned on the fireplace. He takes off his coat, laying it on the chair, then goes to the kitchen and comes back with water. He hands one glass to me.

"I'm sorry if I ruined our evening."

He sits down next to me. "You didn't. How often has this happened to you?"

"At first every tall blonde I saw was her, every phone call that was unknown could be her. It's been a while since I've had that kind of reaction."

"Jamie, do you feel safe with me here?"

His words sober me even more.

"I do. It's just when I saw that woman, little pictures went off in my head. Me fighting with Josh, her abuse at the warehouse and the gun shot...that sound shook me. The picture in my head of your car and if you would be alright."

"There are details of that night we still need to talk about."

"You're right." I pull my legs up under me facing him. "I ran all the way back to the apartment from the accident, trying to think of a way out. When I came around Jordan Hall, she was driving by, looking for me. My chest was burning, but it wasn't from the run—it was from what I had to do. I was about to leave you with her in hopes of keeping you safe until I could figure out a plan."

He takes my hand, lacing his fingers through mine.

"I darted in between buildings because I didn't know what I looked like. I didn't want to bring attention to myself. I made it back to the apartment and slipped inside using the spare key. I couldn't find my phone but grabbed my backpack and I threw a few things inside. I saw the dress from the fundraiser laying on my bed when I got the idea to take your white shirt. My face was throbbing, so I looked in your bathroom mirror and noticed the swelling and dried blood. I couldn't leave like that, so I cleaned the blood off, then pulled on your hoodie, which smelled of you. Your bed was a mess, bringing back the memories of the night before. And that's when I knew I had to see you one last time, to make sure you were alright. I made my way to the hospital where I waited for an opportunity to slip inside your room."

"You were there with me?"

"They had given you something and you were sleeping."

"I remember gasping for air when I arrived at the hospital. I was in and out, but I kept saying your name, hoping someone would listen. But they put a needle in my IV and that's all I remember."

"I picked up your hand, leaving my tears on your skin and on the sheet. I kissed you wanting to keep the feel of your lips on mine. I didn't know where I was going or how far, but I knew this was all I could do to keep you safe, to buy us some time. I heard loud talking outside at the nurse's station. It was Stacey and she was arguing with them because she wanted information about you, but they gave her nothing. I had to leave before she caught me in your room. I took one more kiss, telling you I loved you, then I snuck out, barely hiding behind a door before she rushed in your room with them following. She just wanted to make sure I wasn't with you. Security escorted her out right past me."

"Why New York?"

"I left the hospital that night, then went back to get my truck. I got on the interstate and drove. I just kept crying. I stopped for gas but didn't eat for days. Leaving you was crippling me, tearing me up until I stopped in a parking lot across from a used car lot, just crying. I sold the truck, then bought a train ticket to the last stop on the line. When I got on the train I slept for hours. My body ached and I felt sick and alone. I was grieving again for someone that I loved, but this time it was you."

He pulls me closer to him as my body melts against his.

"Listening to you talk about that night or the days to follow makes me hate her for what she has done to you, to us. We can't let her consume the life we are starting. Jamie, what can I do to help you?"

I look up at him. "Just love me the way you are right now."

"I'm right here. It will take the devil itself to pull me away from you."

"I'm regaining my strength, but it just takes time."

He pulls me over onto his lap. "What can I do for you right now?"

"How about we stay right here where it's warm and cozy?"

He kicks off his shoes and loosens the buttons on his shirt as I turn so he can drape his arm around my body, resting his hand on my stomach. I am safe and so is he. Letting go of the past won't be easy, but with patience it will happen.

Chapter 10

ichael's parents are in town and say they have a huge surprise. Over dinner, they pose a question to us. They ask if we would mind them moving to New York. They've found an apartment not far from us and we can't be happier. Having them so close will give all of us an opportunity to spend more time together. Ruby has joined us for dinner and after their announcement, she gets up and leaves the table, walking to the kitchen. I follow her.

"Ruby, is everything alright?"

"The Tuckers moving here is good news."

"It is."

She takes my hand. "It's time I go home."

"Is it because of their announcement?"

"No. It's just time for me to go back to Texas. We talked about this day."

"I know, but it doesn't mean I want you to go. You're a big part of me, of us all."

"We will always be a part of each other."

I smile at her, holding back tears. "I love you, and I owe you so much."

She takes me in her arms. "You trusted me with your secret, and I got to know Ben, which I am truly thankful. I will never forget this special time we've had together."

"I'm going to miss you."

"You will." She winks. "I will miss you more."

*

The next day feeling bummed about Ruby leaving, I go out shopping for a few items for the loft and for Ben. I ask Mrs. Tucker if she wants to go with me and she agrees, so we leave the three guys at home while we have girl time. We enter a children's boutique and she asks me about Ruby.

"Is she leaving because of us?"

"No. When she came, I knew it would be for a limited time. She has family back in Texas, plus she knows the baby and I are in good hands now. It's time, but I'm still going to miss her."

"She's the sweetest lady and she is so good with Ben. Oh, Jamie look."

She picks up a pair of tiny socks and she seems sad.

I look over at her holding the socks. "Laura, are you alright?"

"I remember when Michael wore little things like this and now he has a little boy. Time goes by so fast." She puts her hand on my arm. "You are so good for him, and he loves you so deeply."

"His love is what I held so close to get through our time apart."

"You both deserve this second chance at happiness."

"Thank you." I pull her into a hug. "We're happy you guys are moving here."

She wipes her eyes and smiles at me, then holds up two pair of socks. "These are my favorite. And thank you—we are looking forward to it. I hope you two don't grow tired of us."

"Are you kidding? Free babysitting…Sunday dinners…we're pumped."

We smile at each other. Our family is growing, and I couldn't be happier.

*

Michael

"Dad, let me do that." I get up to retrieve a clean diaper as my father lays Ben down on the changing table.

"Michael, I run a multi-million dollar company. I think I can handle a poopy diaper."

"Why does hearing that make me laugh?" I step away, folding my arms over my chest watching him. "This is the first time I've seen you do this."

"Well I have to fight Laura to let me do anything with him, but it's cute how she's into being a grandma."

"Did you just say cute?"

He throws a diaper at me. "I can be handy around the house."

"I'm sure you can." When he's done, I take Ben, so Dad can go wash his hands. "Let's get a bottle, little man." I make faces at him as he smiles at me. Every now and then he starts laughing as his belly tightens and his feet kick. I'm sitting on the sofa feeding him when Dad appears.

"Water?"

"Sure." He comes back and sits near us.

Harrison Tucker, hard ass businessman turned mushy grandfather. I like this side of him.

"You're a good father."

"It's all new, but I want to do my best by him."

"You will because you put him first and your love for him is unwavering. I didn't show you enough of that when you were his age or any age."

"Dad, it's all in the past. We're better today. I feel you and Mom are in a better place as well."

"We are. I didn't put her first and I almost lost her."

"I'm sorry, I didn't know."

"It was before Jamie's disappearance. We lost our connection over the years. But we watched you and saw how much you loved Jamie, and it made us realize how important our relationship was and that we needed to fight for it. I have a second chance with her, and you."

"I feel we do." I pick Ben up to burp him. "I'm here for this little guy and for Jamie with everything I got."

Ben burps. "Dude, good job!"

"I have papers to go over with you about the bar. Do you have some time today?"

"Ben, how about some swing time while we discuss the future?"

After 20 minutes of swing time, sleepy time finds Ben. I tuck him into bed touching his fuzzy head with my hand.

"Okay, we talked about most of the details, but I want your mom's special day to be the best, so I still have calls to make. Sleep tight little buddy."

Chapter 11

Jamie

$\mathcal{I}$ 'm heading out to see a new artist today whose medium is in acrylics. I poke my head into Alysse's office.

"Could you get me Trevor Hampton's file? My appointment is at ten and I want to check something before I go."

She rummages through some files on her desk handing it to me. "Here you go."

"Thanks. I'll be back right after the appointment."

"Don't forget we have a 1:00 pm spa date today."

"That's right, we do."

"Your fiancé is very nice to set this up for us."

"He's very thoughtful. I've got to go. See you at Celina's later."

Before walking down the stairs I pull out my phone to send him a text. *"Thank you for my upcoming spa time."* As I get in the car to head out, he texts back. *"My girl deserves the best."* I respond, *"I already have the best, and it's you!"*

*

The artist is seventeen and living in the Bronx with his mother. He's been working with paint since he was seven. I see some good pieces, but I feel he needs some mentoring to pull it all together. We decide to meet again in nine months to evaluate his collection at that time.

I call home to check on Ben before heading to an afternoon of relaxation. I'm told he's enjoying sweet potatoes with pears. The car picks me up and I let Alysse know I am on my way.

*

Celina's is in a trendy part of the city. We enjoy taking walks here on Sundays, stopping for coffee and bagels on our trip back home. Alysse is already waiting for me so we're immediately escorted back and given white robes to change into along with hot pink flip flops for our pedicures. We also have champagne, compliments of Mr. Tucker.

Now it's time for our massages. When done, we're given small sandwiches, along with a tall cold glass of cucumber water. I look over as Alysse pops two in her mouth. I burst out laughing seeing her chipmunk cheeks.

"What? They're so good."

"Yes, they are."

When we've finished our treat, they escort us to the changing room to shower. I slip on a flowered shirtdress and head out to find Alysse texting.

"Who are you texting?"

"Nothing important. Are you ready?"

"Yes."

*

Sitting in the cab we talk about her trip going home. Her parents live in Virginia, and her cousin is getting married. She tells me about some of the restaurants, hotspots, and her friends. She planned a shopping trip with her sister which reminded me of the fun shopping trips at the mall with Susan when we were younger. I've spoken with her a few times since Michael came back into my life, but I need to have her out to visit. I notice Alysse checking her phone again.

"What's so important?"

"We're here."

I look out the window. "Here where?" We're sitting in front of the Trezza Hotel. "Why are we here?"

"An errand."

"What errand would you have to do here?"

She takes my hand. "I love you, but you ask way too many questions. You need to get out of the car because someone is waiting for you."

She looks past me and turns my head to look out the window.

"Your man awaits."

Michael is standing in a tuxedo on the steps to the hotel. I glance back at her and she has a smile stretching as big as I have ever seen.

I look at him as he opens my door. "Babe, why are you wearing a tux? What is going on?"

He kisses my cheek helping me out. "Come with me."

Michael leads me to the elevator still holding on tight to my hand. The doors open and we step inside as he turns to push the button. I peek around him to see the number, but he blocks me.

"How was your spa day?"

"It was wonderful, but I don't understand what's going on."

The elevator stops and he guides me out along a small hall and through a double door to a space filled with round tables covered in white linen tablecloths. Vases full of pale pink and white peonies fragrance the air. I turn to Michael who is down on one knee.

"Jamie, will you marry me, tonight?"

I look back at the decorations realizing they're from my book of sketches for our wedding.

"This is for us?"

"It is."

He stands up, taking my hands in his. "Jamie, I love you with all that I have. You are all I think about and the only woman I will ever need. Will you take the next step with me tonight?"

"Yes, I will."

He pulls me close as our heads rest against one another taking in the moment. My hand finds the back of his neck, pulling his lips close to mine.

"I love you." I kiss him. "Is this really happening?"

"It is."

"I can't believe you did all of this."

"I had help. The day after our walk with Ben in the park I contacted Alysse and she copied your book for me. I wanted you to have everything you dreamed about."

I step away from him, admiring the table settings when little lights turn on, holding us in the most romantic space I've ever seen. I stand looking up at the stars as his arms wrap around me.

"In the open, this close to the stars I feel my parents are with us. I know that's a crazy thing to say."

"It's not." He turns me around. "I have a lot of surprises, but first Alysse is going to take you to the suite and help you get ready. Savannah has given you two dress options from the sketches you provided. If you don't like something or just want something different, just let Alysse know and she will text me. I won't see you again until you walk down the aisle to me and become mine."

I smile, touching his cheek with my finger. "I've always been yours."

We kiss again when we hear Alysse clear her throat. "So, are we having a wedding?"

"She's taking a gigantic leap not knowing the details, but yes we are getting married," Michael says.

She gives us a hug. "I kept a huge secret from you. Are you mad?"

"No. Thank you for helping make our day come true."

"Alysse will take you from here. I have a few more things to finalize."

She pulls me away from him. I squeeze her hand showing my excitement.

"You're strong, ouch." She giggles.

"I can't believe this is real!"

"Are you sure about this?"

"I would have married him weeks ago, but I knew he wanted a wedding and deep down so did I. What other surprises does he have planned?"

"You won't get me to reveal any secrets about tonight. Michael would hunt me down if I ruined this for you. Besides your fiancé, soon-to-be husband, put a lot of effort into making this a day to remember. So don't ask me."

We stop at a door that has a big white ribbon on it that says, "Bride's Suite." She puts in the key and my eyes take in a room full of flowers, food, and bottles of champagne.

"Oh my gosh!"

"Pretty great huh? Champagne for the bride?"

"Sure." I take it all in traveling to the bedroom to see garment bags and boxes. She joins me with two glasses.

"Thank you."

"Now everything you'll need for tonight is right in this bedroom, except for the groom of course." She walks me into the bathroom. "Since we've already been pampered, next is hair and makeup which is being done by Mica, from Simone's Hair Salon. Are you ready?"

"If it gets me down the aisle to Michael faster, yes."

*

I sit in the bathroom as Mica finishes with my hair. I've been eyeing a small box with my name on it sitting on the counter when Alysse joins us.

"Should I open it?"

"Yes. There are little things everywhere."

She hands me the box.

I pull off the blue ribbon and lift the lid. Inside is a note that says, "Something Blue." I pull out a pale blue lace garter and under it another note along with another garter that is white. The note says, "For keeps."

"One to throw, one to keep. I love them both."

"When your makeup is done, we'll look at the dresses. No one has seen them except for Savannah."

"I feel like I'm in a movie, but the outcome will be my life."

As my hair and makeup are now done, it's on to unveil the dresses. The first garment bag holds a mermaid style off-the-shoulder white chiffon dress and the second has a chiffon halter neck floor length gown with lace in the back. Both are beautiful. Alysse opens the tops of the shoeboxes and I see another box with a pink ribbon.

"What is this?" I untie the ribbon and pull off the top to find white tissue paper with a note that reads, "Something New." Inside is a pair of white lace underwear.

"He likes lingerie."

"Got to love that in a man. So which dress?"

"The halter style with the t-strap platforms with pearl accents. Will you help me put it on?"

"Yes, of course."

We stand in front of the mirror side by side.

"Savannah is really gifted. Jamie, you look so beautiful and the fit is amazing."

We hear voices in the other room only to see Mrs. Tucker and Ruby walk in the bedroom. Both look so pretty in their gowns. Mrs. Tucker is blotting her eyes. She reaches me first.

"Oh, my goodness, Jamie."

"No crying or all of this makeup will run. You look amazing."

"It's been hard to keep this a secret, but Michael wanted you to be surprised."

"He accomplished that—I had no idea."

Ruby is next to her, wiping her cheeks.

"Ruby, don't cry."

"Happy tears sweetheart, happy tears. Your parents are smiling with pride right now."

I fan my face, holding back my own tears. "I'm glad you're here today."

"I wouldn't have missed this."

"Where's Ben?"

"He is with the boys. Harrison has him."

Mrs. Tucker comes over with a box. "He and I wanted you to have something borrowed from our family. He gave me these earrings when we got married, would you wear them today?"

She pulls out a pair of diamond teardrop earrings.

"Oh Laura, they're exquisite. I would love to wear them, thank you."

Alysse comes in announcing the photographer is here. "Are you ready?"

I smile at all three ladies. "I am."

Chapter 12

Jamie

I'm standing in a hall waiting for the ceremony to begin, with Ruby by my side to walk me down the aisle. Alysse is fussing with my dress. I hold my bouquet up to my nose thinking how I wish my parents could be here, when I see a locket among the petals. Opening it, I find a picture of my parents inside. I look at Ruby.

"Where did this come from?"

"Michael gave me the locket and when I flew home, I found a picture of them on their wedding day in the church archives. It's your something old, mixed with new. I hope you like it."

"Thank you." I lean over, hugging her. "I don't know how much longer I'm going to hold out without crying buckets of tears today."

"Cry all you want, because there are more surprises on the other side of the door."

I look at her feeling a little nervous. I just need to see Michael or Ben to calm myself down. Music begins to play, and I grab Ruby's hand, giving it a gentle squeeze.

The door opens, and the rooftop space is twinkling with lights and flower petals line my path to Michael. I'm looking for him when Alysse slides in front of us, holding out her arm as Pete steps up. I blink making sure it's him. He smiles, then winks at me as they walk away from us.

We step a little closer to the door when I see another mauve dress beside us. It's Susan! She gives me a kiss on my cheek.

"I wasn't going to miss this."

She holds out her arm to Stan, who smiles at me with a nod of his head as they walk down the aisle in front of us. Suddenly, I notice the people sitting in the chairs that I didn't see before. They are filled with new friends, and people from our past at Hopson. My chest starts to feel tight. I haven't spoken to them since leaving, but they're here, here for us. One more couple takes the aisle before we do. It's Max and Maci! Oh my God, she's beautiful and very pregnant. She blows me a kiss and Max smiles.

The feelings I have whirling through my body are getting out of control. I need to get to him soon. I blow out a breath, take in another, then repeat.

"It's our turn Jamie, ready?"

All I can do is nod in agreement. The people staring back at us as we walk down the aisle are the ones who had his back when I left, then there are the ones who supported me when I arrived in New York. But from the looks of all gathered here tonight, they are still very much a part of both of our lives.

I look up to finally see Michael standing in his black tux, holding Ben who is wearing a matching one. I smile looking at the two most important people in my life. Both handsome, calming my every nerve. Michael reaches up, wiping a tear off his face. He is a beautiful soul, a man I adore and love so deeply. Ruby and I make it up to where they're standing, and I reach over, kissing Ben on his head, then look up at Michael.

"Hi."

"Hey gorgeous."

He hands Ben over to Mrs. Tucker. When the officiant asks who gives this woman, Ruby holds her hand out to Robert and Savannah who both stand up to join us. In unison they all answer, "We do."

Each one gives me a kiss on my cheek. There are no holding tears back now. I was once a grieving girl arriving in Hopson with no family, but now I have many. Ruby, Savannah, and Robert have all stepped up to stand in for my parents. I could not be prouder than I am right now to have them along with me on this special day.

I turn to Michael and see his dad as the best man, Pete, Stan, and Max as groomsmen. I hand my bouquet off to Susan, and then turn back to my groom. He touches my cheek catching tears.

I mouth the words, "I love you" and he does the same.

The officiant leads us in a prayer, then begins to tell the guests we are going to say our own vows. Michael looks terrified. I let out a nervous giggle.

He leans in to whisper. "I forgot to tell you this part."

"I'm speaking about you, it will be easy."

The officiant speaks to me. "Jamie, you may begin."

I take Michael's hands in mine.

"Michael. You fixed my broken heart, twice. You filled it with hope and happiness by loving me the way you do every minute of every day. I look into your eyes and I see a man who is strong, caring, and gentle. I want to hold your hand in life, while living out our dreams together as a family. I love your smile, your sense of humor, and the look you give me setting off butterflies in my stomach. I love the way you know what I need before I do. With your arms wrapped around me I feel safe and protected. I will support you, be here for you, and go through life by your side as our story continues. I love you with all my heart, forever and always."

He smiles at me as a tear trickles down his cheek. I wipe it off then squeeze his hand.

"Jamie. When you arrived on my doorstep back in college soaked from all the rain, I thought you were gorgeous. My heart fell for you immediately and I wanted to know everything about you. When I look into your eyes, I feel your love for me. It's honest and pure. Your spirit lights up mine, making me stronger. You are a beautiful person and I choose you for my partner in this life and beyond. I want to be the husband you deserve and the man you desire. As you just said, our story will continue. You are my best friend. I love you with all my heart, forever and always."

He leans in to kiss me when he is stopped by the officiant as our friends and family chuckle at his eagerness.

"Not yet Michael, we have a few more things to cover."

He smiles, a little embarrassed. "The rings."

We both turn to retrieve our rings.

"Jamie, do you take Michael to be your husband?"

"I do." I slip on his ring.

"Michael, do you take Jamie to be your wife?"

"I do." He slips on my ring.

"With the exchanging of vows and rings, I now pronounce you husband and wife. Michael, you can now kiss your bride."

He does just that. We seal our union with a kiss. Everyone claps and cheers as we turn to face them.

The officiant speaks again. "Please stand and welcome Mr. and Mrs. Michael and Jamie Tucker."

We kiss again, then begin our walk down the aisle. As we reach the hall, he brings my chin up to his, kissing me this time just for us.

"Mrs. Tucker, are you up for more?"

"With you Mr. Tucker, I'm up for more always."

"Any regrets so far?"

"How could I? This was such a labor of love. It's beautiful. How did you get everyone here?"

"I filled in those I knew you would like to share this day with, told them about our privacy, and they were all in right away."

"How lucky was I to knock on your door that day at Hopson?"

He pulls me closer to him. "Not luck, destiny."

"You are a sweet romantic wrapped up in hard muscle." I pick up his hand with his wedding band. "Now you're all mine."

He touches my cheek as we kiss again.

Chapter 13

Jamie

Hand in hand, we're the last ones to enter the reception after taking pictures. I lean into his arm.

"Maybe we can plan a honeymoon soon."

He stops. "How about one now?"

I look at him. "Are we?"

"My next surprise. Tomorrow we leave for a week on a tropical island hidden away from the world."

"But I can't leave Ben. He's so small and my job requires me to be here for the next week or so because Alysse is going out of town to visit her parents."

"That was all a lie. But a good one. I spoke with Robert. You're cleared to be gone for a week. My parents will keep Ben at our apartment. I want this to work, but only if you are okay with it."

"You've thought of everything. Let's do it."

He kisses me again.

We're announced to our guests and enter to one of our favorite songs. Our guests have been given drinks and our bridesmaids and groomsmen are now cleared to go and have some fun. Laura is standing near us holding Ben. I reach out to take him.

"You look so cute in your tux." I kiss his head.

"He's a good baby and I have a daughter in-law."

"And I a mother in-law."

Michael steps in to kiss her cheek.

"Congratulations son."

"Thanks, Mom."

His dad steps in, kissing me on my cheek and then shaking his son's hand. "Congratulations to you both."

"Thank you."

I hand Ben to Michael, who tosses him in the air a bit, then hands Ben to his father. Michael takes hold of my hand.

"Who do you want to see first?"

"Pete."

We spot him coming to us before those words even leave my mouth. Michael drops my hand, so I can hug him.

"I've missed your pretty face. I'm so glad you are okay," Pete says.

"Thank you for being there for him. I will always regret the hurt I caused."

He stops me.

"We all know you never would have done what you did if there was another way. You protected him, then you took care of Ben. Now you both have a second chance. I never wanted to believe you were…"

"She's right here, beautiful as ever," Michael says.

Pete hugs Michael. "Congratulations."

"Thanks Pete."

"I met Ben, good solid boy."

We both smile knowing that is very true.

He touches my cheek. "You both will be just fine. You have lots of people to speak with so I'm going to get a drink. I love you both."

I look up at Michael and smile. "I missed him."

"He missed you."

Stan approaches, shaking his head at me and smiling. "You look stunning."

Michael shakes his hand. "Thank you, I feel pretty good."

"Not you, dude." He leans over to kiss my cheek. "Tell me now—we can leave and run far away from this monkey."

"Stan, I see you haven't changed." I give him a hug.

"Jeff sends his love, but business had him out of the country. We're glad you're okay. It's good to see him happy and the two of you together."

"Yes, I agree. Michael told me about Sophie, how is she?"

"Good. She's in her last year at Hopson. We're moving to Washington State after graduation."

"For a job?"

"Yes, hers. We have something pretty special."

"I'm happy for you both."

He punches Michael. "Be good to her, or I'll be back for you."

Michael is smiling as Stan walks to the bar. "It's good to see him. How about some food?"

He snags us some crab bites along with a glass of champagne when Susan finds us, silently screaming with happiness.

"Jamie, you are so pretty, and this dress hugs every curve I always tried to get you to show." She hugs me. "I'm so happy for you both."

Then she hugs Michael. "Very romantic move on your part. Look how much she's smiling."

"I would do anything to keep her smiling." He takes my glass. "Let me get us a refill; you two catch up."

I follow him with my eyes as he walks away, not wanting to let him out of my sight.

"He is my knight in shining armor."

He looks back at me and I blow him a kiss before he bumps into Robert.

"Susan, where is your doctor?"

She points across the room. "Right there. All five foot eleven inches of him. He's flipped my world upside down. The night Ben was born, who knew I would find a keeper? He's smart, cute, and I just love him."

"Yes, you do."

"I constantly think about him, but you know what that's like. Ben seems happy and that tuxedo…he's crushing the cute factor. You're finally at peace having them both with you, aren't you?"

"I am. They keep me strong."

She pulls me into a hug. "I love you, your husband, and my nephew."

"We love you too. Now go find Thomas, while I find food."

Michael hands me my glass back, popping a shrimp in my mouth and sealing it with a kiss. As I chew, I make faces at how good it tastes.

"Please tell me there are more of those."

"These are just the appetizers, more food is coming. Let's go speak to more of our guests as I snag us more."

We made our rounds to speak with everyone, but it also gives me a chance to really see all the things that he's put into place. I love speaking with Meredith, who is now giving Ben a bottle while Pete looks over them along with Ruby. Alysse is having some fun with Randall, her plus one for the wedding, and I learn that Robert and Savannah gifted our wedding cake. I stand for a moment just taking everything in, looking out over all the people who are attending our special day, and smile. Family is more than blood relatives—it's the people who have your back, who show up in support of you. We are very blessed.

*

A couple of hours into the celebration Ben grows tired and Ruby excuses herself, taking him upstairs for the evening. We're enjoying some of the tasty creations when I take a moment to look at my husband. I reach over and place my hand on his knee. He stops chewing, turning himself towards me.

"Time to depart?"

"Not yet, but that offer is very tempting." He'd taken off his jacket when we went to dance. "You're very handsome especially in my favorite shirt."

He leans over, kissing me. "I wore it just for you."

"Tonight has been magical, a dream come true."

"You're glowing. Is it the lights or me?"

"Definitely you."

He picks up a chunk of roast beef, popping it in my mouth. I chew the tender meat mumbling how good it is.

"You still have one more person to meet." He points past me.

"I thought we spoke to everyone," I say, looking towards the door. Then I see Caleb.

Michael stands, taking my hand. "Let's go see him."

Caleb seems to have come alone, dressed in a blue suit and holding a wrapped gift. Michael greets him first with a handshake, then a hug.

"Man, I'm so glad you made it."

I wait to hear his voice, one I truly missed. We've spoken on the phone, but not face to face in a long time.

"No way would I have missed this. It's not every day your two best friends get married." He looks past Michael at me smiling.

I step over to him, sliding my arms around his neck. "I can't believe you're here."

"I can't believe you're married."

Michael touches my elbow. "I'm going to call up and check on Ben so you both can talk." He kisses me, then leaves.

"Caleb, let's get a drink."

I reach out my hand to him and he takes it as we walk to the bar.

Chapter 14

Jamie

s we wait for our drinks, I can't help but look at my friend and he does the same.

"Caleb, it's really good to see you."

He rubs his forehead. "I can't believe you're standing right here. Michael filled me in on what you went through. If I had only known what lengths she was willing to go to, maybe I could have stopped her."

"I never thought Stacey would go that far. The threats she made against Michael, his parents, and the baby. Everything she told me about being my sister, and then Josh."

He lays a hand on mine. "What you did took courage. You need to stop feeling guilty."

"It's hard. I put him through so much, and then kept his son from him."

"No, you kept him safe, and then continued to sacrifice your own happiness to keep your son safe. He doesn't blame you. He loves you and you both look good together, you always have. On a scale from one to ten, how happy are you?"

"Way past ten."

He tips up his drink. "It shows."

"Well look at you. What, no woman on your arm?"

"No. All of my energy is with Eli, no time for a woman."

"Do you have a current picture?"

"Are you kidding me?" He pulls out his phone, showing me pictures of his son.

"Caleb, he's beautiful," I say. "Ben was down earlier, but I would love for you to see him before you leave."

"Me too."

A song begins playing as a smile appears on my face. I look around for my husband, who is standing in the middle of the dance floor, one hand in his pocket waiting for me.

"Excuse me Caleb."

"Go, go."

Everyone gathers as his hand extends to me. "Hey you."

"Do you remember it?"

"I do. You sang this to me in 42 after we got together as a couple."

"It's how I felt about you then and especially now."

His lips meet mine and I feel the connection deep inside. We both know what it took to get to where we are today, making this day even bigger. He tucks my hand close to his chest and begins to sing the song and I feel every word.

After more drinks, cake, and throwing of the garter (which is caught by Stan) and throwing the bouquet (which is caught by Tanner), we begin to say goodbye to all our guests. I've loved every minute of our wedding, but now I want to just be with Michael.

Stealing kisses in the hall and holding hands, we reach our door eyeing a sign that says, DO NOT DISTURB, JUST MARRIED! I look over at him.

"You?"

He shakes his head, then scoops me up in his arms, using the key to open the door and then walking us through. It's the same room, but the decorations are different. I look around.

"Wow, this is awesome."

"Compliments of Susan."

We walk to the table and I grab a chocolate covered strawberry, holding one up for him. He takes it in one bite while kissing me. I giggle, wiping off my mouth. He pops another bottle, filling two glasses.

"To my exquisite wife who captured my heart tonight in this dress."

"To my charming husband who was looking super-hot in his tuxedo."

He kneels in front of me, setting down his glass. "May I help you with your shoes?"

"You may."

He takes my leg and pulls my dress up over my knee. Setting my foot on his knee, he runs fingers up my leg, leaving a kiss on my thigh.

Looking up, he smiles. "You're wearing my garter."

"I am. It's very special."

He hooks his fingers under the lace, pulling it off and placing it in his pocket. He goes about undoing the strap of the first shoe, then on to the next one.

"May I help you out of anything else?"

"Everything I have on is yours to take whenever you want."

He takes my hand and leads me into the bedroom where we find the bed covered in flower petals. I set down my glass. He backs me up against the edge of the bed where we both fall onto it as the flowers scatter around us. He props himself up on one elbow, dropping petals on me as I blow a few at him.

"Let me get the pins from your hair."

He pulls me up on my knees as he sits behind me, removing one at a time. My hands are not idle as I touch him wherever I can reach. He tries to keep it together, but my attempts prove to throw him over the edge.

"Forget the pins."

*

I'm now hypnotized by his fingers on my bare skin, lost in this wonderful connection between us. He leans over me.

"I guess our rowdy behavior mixed with the flower petals has colored your skin like tiny tattoos." He removes a couple, and then moves down to my thigh, peeling one off and kissing the spot.

I curl towards him. "You know what that does to me."

"I do, and I never want to stop making you feel that way."

I run my fingers through his hair, pulling him to me. "I love that you won't."

*

After sleeping for a few hours, I slip out of bed to wash my face and pull on my bridal robe. When I come back into the bedroom, he's gone. Walking out into the living room I find him looking at his phone.

"Who are you calling?"

"Checking my phone in case Ruby called."

"Turning off the father switch isn't easy, is it?"

"No. Why are you up, need fuel?" He pulls me into his arms.

"Yes, actually, I'm hungry."

His eyebrow raises, implying he has something in mind. "I got us covered."

He pulls out a couple of containers from the fridge where I see miniatures of what we had at the wedding.

"That all looks so good. Let me get us some water."

We park ourselves on the sofa outside on the balcony, tasting the little bite size goodies and talking over special moments from the wedding.

"You do understand why I'm having a few reservations about leaving Ben, right?"

"I do, and I understand it's hard for you to step back and allow others to do what only you have done. Jamie, I understand."

"It's always been the unknown that scares me."

"It's your love and protective nature that has kept us all safe, but I need you to let me help."

I stand up walking to the balcony, then turn back to him. "I know you've done everything you can to make this work for us. I do trust you to take care of us. I want to go."

"Are you sure?"

"I am positively positive."

He joins me at the balcony. "Ben will be under the loving protection of his grandparents who are both fiercely in love with their first grandchild."

"This is true. Now, what about clothes?"

"I took care of it all." He goes inside and returns with two bags.

"We're going away for a week and that's all you packed?"

"I packed a new bikini for you."

"I'm to live in a bikini all week?"

"No, not the whole week. I prefer you be naked most of the time."

"Well, naked it is. This means you too."

"How about we start now?"

He reaches for my robe and I back away. He cuts his eyes at me. I feel if I don't want to expose myself on the balcony, I should run, which I do. He takes off after me as I let out a scream, running around the sofa when he reaches out and catches me up close to him. I pull my hair off my face to see his excited grin.

"I think I'm about to be naked."

"I think you're right."

Chapter 15

Jamie

I lay in bed this morning admiring my shiny new wedding band. I shake my head reliving last night, only to turn towards the bathroom as the shower stops. I sit up in bed just in time to watch him wrap a towel around his waist as he runs his fingers through his wet hair.

"Good morning Mrs. Tucker, did you sleep well?" he asks.

I crawl out of bed and meet him in the bathroom. Running my finger down the few lucky drops of water left behind to fall over his skin, I pop my finger in my mouth.

"No, but yes."

He bends over to kiss me. "Sounds like our next week will be the same."

I disappear around the corner to use the bathroom. "How many people stayed last night?"

"All of the out of towners and then others came back this morning for the brunch."

I flush and come out to start the shower. "Did you pack me clothes for today?"

"I'll lay them out while you shower. I just received a message that Ben is awake and ready to see his parents. I thought we could spend some time together before seeing everyone else."

"Then I'll hurry."

Awhile later, I cut off the dryer and hear my two guys in the other room. They appear in the doorway of the bathroom.

"Tell Mom what you did with Ruby this morning?" Michael says to Ben.

"What did you do?" I reach over, kissing his hand and Michael leans down for me to take him.

"He army crawled?" Michael has a look of confusion on his face.

"I read about that. They lay on their bellies, pulling themselves across the floor with their arms."

"Really?"

I cuddle him close to me. "Yes, and we missed it."

Now the look on Michael's face is a sad one, one of disappointment.

"Don't be sad, Daddy. He was with someone who loves him who I am sure gave wonderful words of encouragement, just like we would."

Michael's brow relaxes as he bends to pick up the pacifier. "This is true. I'm going to heat his bottle, I'll meet you in the living room."

I spread out a towel on the floor where I place him until I finish applying mascara, then off to the bedroom to get dressed.

Michael has the bottle ready by the time I'm done. "Here Momma, you want to feed him?"

"I would love to. You never told me last night where our travels will take us today."

"I did not. My dad picked the destination and Mom saw to the details."

"But you know?"

"Yes."

"So, I won't know until I get there?"

"No."

I turn to Ben. "I guess that will do."

*

An hour with Ben goes by so fast and we're now in the elevator heading to our brunch. The doors open with our family and friends on the other side cheering for us. Laura retrieves Ben, allowing us to welcome our guests and maybe even grab mimosas, which leads me to our hostess, Alysse.

She ushers us to a table with flowers and items from the wedding along with two plates, piled high with food, along with a tray of fruits. There are mini biscuits with ham, roast beef, and chicken salad.

"Where did you find the time to fix all of this and prepare for your vacation home next week?"

She looks at Michael surprised by my comment, but he knows I'm playing. Her mouth flies open wordlessly, then I smile.

"There were a lot of secrets to keep from you, which was hard. Are you okay?"

"I definitely am. Thank you for playing along with his master plan to take me away. I appreciate you clearing the calendar at work."

"You both deserve some one on one time. Besides you and I work together to make things happen. Now this delightful spread is for you both. Oh, and we have a brownie tower just over there."

"We keep this up, running will be on my agenda for the next month," I laugh.

Michael puts his arm around me. "Not away from me I hope."

"Never away from you."

We kiss, and everyone cheers. We take this moment to thank everyone for attending the wedding and for being at the brunch to continue the celebration of our union. Then we release everyone to eat.

After an ample amount of food, we go to speak with our guests. The first stop is Max and Maci. We spoke to them last night, but want more information on their new arrival. She waddles towards us with her arms out wide, hugging me first.

"Jamie, I know I told you last night, but it's so good to have you back with us. You are absolutely glowing."

"Me! Look at you."

"I feel like a pregnant giraffe."

"You're beautiful."

Max places his hands on her hips. "She hasn't missed one day of work, with everything in its place at home and at work."

Michael chimes in. "I have to agree with Jamie."

She smiles. "You're sweet, thank you. So where is this secret honeymoon?"

We all look at Michael.

"Not saying."

"What? How do you expect her to travel without knowing what to pack?"

"She doesn't need anything."

She looks puzzled as the three of us grin. "You can't be naked in public. What if she wants to shop or go for that run?"

Max and Michael look at each other as she hits her husband in the arm.

"It's all good, Maci," I say. "He says he packed a bikini."

Michael slips an arm around me. "I've taken care of everything."

She crosses her arms. "Are you serious?"

Max takes her arm. "Maci, they'll be fine. Naked isn't a bad choice."

She rolls her eyes at him and walks towards the buffet. We step away to greet more of our guests. Pete has Michael at the table talking business, so I take a moment to speak with Caleb.

"Hey, can we talk?"

"Of course."

We find ourselves on one of the balconies just outside, that overlooks the city.

"Thanks again for making the trip out here for us."

"This I was not going to miss. I'm happy for you both."

"Michael is coming to Hopson soon on 42 business. I want to come back with him and bring Ben. I can't wait to see Eli in person."

"I'd like that. Who knew we would be an aunt and uncle?"

My arms slide around him. "I love that we are."

Caleb leaves and I stand looking at Michael, who is talking with Stan. Susan appears in front of me holding up her hand, which holds a new diamond. I grab it.

"What is this?! When did it happen?"

"He said he's had the ring for a few weeks waiting for that perfect moment. After hearing your vows last night and seeing all the love that exudes from you two, he asked me after we returned to our room last night. He had champagne and my favorite chocolate waiting on the balcony. It was beautiful and romantic with the lights from the city below."

We hug each other tight.

"I'm so happy for you. He is a lucky man."

"Thank you and yes he is. I can't wait until you return so we can start planning. I'm thinking destination wedding in Vegas and soon."

"Sounds fabulous."

"Michael had me in town for a secret meeting a few weeks ago when he was planning all of this. Alysse was there along with his mom. We've all been sneaking around, making calls and hoping you would be surprised when the day arrived."

"Well, I was."

"I'm not going to keep you all to myself any longer and leave Thomas to the waitress in the ponytail," she says, before taking my hands in hers. "You and Michael deserve all of this and more. I love you."

"I love you too."

I go in and find our son in his father's arms. In just the few months they've been together, he and Ben have secured a place with each other, a bond that I know will never be broken.

"The two cutest guys here."

"Are you about ready to go?"

"You have our schedule; do we have some more time with him before he goes home with your parents?"

"Yes."

"Then it's time to say goodbye to our guests."

The people who came to share in our wedding mean so much to both of us. They were with us when we were friends and when we fell in love. They've been with us through all the pain when we were apart and now they can see we've made it back together and have a son. I will forever be thankful for each of them.

Back in the hotel room, I gather a few toiletries from the bathroom while Michael has Ben on the floor in the living room. He starts to speak to his son in a low tone, saying we won't be gone long and to please not do anything monumental until Momma gets back. He says he loves him and that he's going to miss him.

I step over squatting next to them.

"Daddy having a hard time saying goodbye?"

Michael sits against the sofa patting the space between his legs for me. As I sit, Ben rolls over on his back chewing on a turtle.

"They have all the important numbers and I took them over to meet his pediatrician."

"You really did do everything to make this work. My husband is a genius!"

"I'm motivated," he says, kissing me.

Chapter 16

Jamie

We change flights once and then board a smaller plane to our secluded destination. The drive to our site which takes about 30 minutes. We pull up to what looks like a small cottage warmed with the glow of lights inside and lining the path to the front door. There is a blue front door and I am once again scooped up by my husband.

"Will you do this with every threshold we cross?"

"I will." He kisses me, setting me down in front of him.

We notice a gentleman standing near us wearing khakis and a blue button up shirt, who introduces himself.

"I am Roger, your concierge for the week."

"We are the Tuckers. Michael and Jamie," Michael introduces us.

I extend my hand. "Nice to meet you Roger."

He smiles. "Let me first say, congratulations."

In unison we both say thank you.

"I will let you check out the cottage and see if everything is to your liking and then meet you back here to fill you in on details about your week."

We proceed to walk through our cottage, noticing the easy-going style of furniture with lots of pastels, whites, and tans. It has one bedroom with a huge bed surrounded by windows covered in plantation shutters. The bathroom is small with a stand-up shower and a huge tub looking out over the beach. We head back out to the living room where Roger has opened the doors allowing a light breeze to infiltrate the room. I look at Michael.

"It's beautiful. Our own peace of heaven."

He slides his hand around my waist. "The beach is spectacular."

Roger clears his throat. "Is everything to your liking?"

Michael turns to him. "Yes, I think so."

"There is a stocked fridge, bikes, and a car. I can get anything else to you if you call me. I can make reservations for meals, or have food prepared here. My number is next to the phone and I am available 24 hours a day."

A woman in a blue dress comes out of the kitchen.

"This is Maggie. She will be the one preparing food for you, picnic lunches, or late night snacks."

She steps forward holding out her hand. "Nice to meet you, Mr. and Mrs. Tucker."

I take her hand. "It's nice to meet you too."

Michael addresses Roger as Maggie slips back into the kitchen. "We have a few excursions planned already, where do I find information about them?"

Roger takes him to a table by the door, going over a notebook with him. Maggie reappears with a tray.

"I thought you might be hungry, so I made a couple of things for you both. We figured tonight you would want to relax and be alone."

I smile at her, looking over the tray. "Thank you."

"You can call me anytime. Will there be anything else?"

"No, ma'am, we're fine."

They both say their goodbyes leaving us alone. After locking the door, Michael comes over to me. I'm holding two glasses of island punch.

"To our second night as a married couple."

"Aren't you a little curious about clothing options?"

"No, you have me covered or not covered. Pretty self-explanatory." I smile over my glass at him.

"The bags we brought are basically for us to take clothes home." He holds out his hand. "Come with me."

"A reveal," I say, putting down my punch.

He looks over his shoulder, smiling. He places me in front of the closet to wait while he asks me to close my eyes. I hear the doors open in front of me.

"Open your eyes."

A variety of clothes hang in the closet. Then he takes me to the dresser, showing me more. Not just for me, but for him as well.

"Did you do all of this?" I pick up a pair of small lacy underwear holding them in front of me.

"Those, yes. The dresses, shorts, and shirts, etc., were picked out by Savannah. As much as I prefer you naked, we might be going out, so you will need a few things."

"We are living in a fairy tale."

He kisses me. "No this is real life, our life." He walks past me to the bathroom after grabbing something out of one of the drawers for himself. "I'll meet you on the deck after your clothes tour."

"Sounds good."

*

After washing my face, I change into a long white maxi dress that is held together only by the fabric wrapped around my chest. I go in search of my husband and find him standing with his back to me looking at the ocean. The smell of flowers surrounds me, taking over my senses and relaxing every muscle in my body. The sun has set, leaving the water to be illuminated by the moon. The light breeze touches my skin.

Michael is wearing khaki shorts and a pullover white t-shirt. He's barefoot, resting his hands on the rail. I move in and wrap my arms around his waist.

"Hey you."

He turns to me. "Beautiful, good choice."

"I think with one pull it will fall right off."

He hands me a glass. "So, one pull and I have you back to my original plan."

I take a sip. "Yep."

"Tomorrow you'll able to see the beach and everything we have at our disposal for the next week." He pulls out a chair for me.

"Our own private paradise?"

He points at some lights to the right. "Those are our closest neighbors."

"A quiet spot for a honeymoon."

"Well it depends on how much noise we create."

"Do we have sunscreen?"

"Yes." He reaches over, pulling my chair closer to his. "I want to be able to touch you all week."

"How is it that one comment like that makes my brain think of things to do to you?"

Before I can have another thought, I'm sitting on his lap, enjoying kissing under the stars when he proposes a question.

"Moonlight swim?"

"Sure."

When he reaches the water's edge, he starts peeling out of his shirt, his eyes on me. He pulls at my tied dress as I catch it, smiling. He takes off his shorts, heading for the water; the sight of him makes my cheeks feel warm. I look around needing to embrace our privacy, so I let the dress fall on the sand joining him in the ocean. He swims to me.

"I know you've been skinny dipping before."

"Yes, but this time will be different."

Chapter 17

Jamie

The next morning while we eat a light breakfast of bagels and fresh fruit, we talk over our day, then call Roger to set up our spot on the beach and Maggie to pack a picnic lunch along with a cooler of beer.

There is much to see today that we couldn't last night, but there's no need to rush to see it all as we have all week. Walking down to the water, the sand under my feet feels soft. We have a couple of umbrellas, lounge chairs, and all the items we requested to have a relaxing day. I pick up the sunscreen and walk to his chair.

"May I?" I ask, holding up the tube.

"Yes, then I will do you."

I rub the lotion over his skin not wanting to miss a spot. When I'm done, he does the same for me. Landing in the chair next to him, I confess my call from earlier.

"I hope you don't mind, but I called home already."

"Why would I mind? I don't expect you to cut ties with Ben. He's our son and we have unusual circumstances to always consider. Besides, I texted this morning as well."

We look at each other, feeling the same way about being separated from him, but promise to relax and just be newlyweds.

I wake to find the chair next to me empty. I pull on my coverup, feeling hungry as I reach for a bottle of water. All I can hear is the occasional bird and water lapping against the beach. No wonder I slept so well—it's a tranquil setting.

"Hey gorgeous, how was your nap?"

I stretch. "Wonderful. Where did you go?"

"Lunch is ready."

I take his hand as we walk back to our cottage. The first thing I see is a table set up with fresh fruit, fish with veggies, and a drink chilling in a glass.

"What's inside this beauty?"

"Papaya fruit infused with three types of alcohol, one that is produced on the island."

"Looks refreshing." I take a sip. "Incredible."

He pulls out my chair. "Let's eat."

"How long was I asleep?"

"No clocks in paradise."

I giggle. "That's fair."

We dig into our lunch leaving nothing untouched.

"Roger told me about a waterfall down the beach, do you want to go for a walk after lunch?"

"Sounds magical."

He pulls a brochure out of his pocket. "I planned our excursion for tomorrow."

He hands it to me, and my eyes light up. "Horseback riding on the beach, are you serious?"

"I am."

"Riding on the beach will be another first for me. Have you done it before?"

"I have."

"I need to figure out more creative firsts for you."

"Hmm, really."

"You've had more experiences than me, so I'll give it some thought and get back to you."

"I'm looking forward to it."

We finish lunch and take off on our journey to the waterfall. Roger was right, it is spectacular! I've never seen anything like it. From the sound of the water down the side of the mountain to the rainbow of flowers laying in a bed of green foliage, it all leaves us speechless. We're able to catch a couple of species of birds that wear an array of different colors with long beaks. We hike the path up as far as we can, then sit and take in the scenery below us. I'm again in awe at the sight of this place. We take some pictures, then I stand, looking down at the water below us.

Getting an idea, I turn to him. "Have you ever jumped into the water below a waterfall? Do you think it's safe?"

"Roger said it is, and no, I have not. Are you sure you want to?"

I take his hand and nod. We jump feet first, hitting the water with a splash, then popping back to the surface in no time. I come up gasping for air and shaking my head when I feel his hands pull me over to him.

"Are you okay?"

"Yes, that was exhilarating!"

"That was my first. I can't believe we jumped from way up there."

He's smiling at me with a goofy grin when I realize why. My top is gone. I start splashing him and the sound of his laughter warms my heart.

"Your plan to keep me out of my clothes has worked, again."

His hand wraps around my neck, pulling me close. "I love your willingness to do something new even when it costs you your top."

"Team Tucker all the way." I raise my hand in victory.

Back at our beach we go snorkeling, finding schools of fish, a variety of shells, and then return to land to lie in hammocks and watch the sun disappear before us. We choose to stay in tonight, listen to music, and dine on fish tacos with fresh pineapple salsa and guacamole. Laying on the sofa with my head in his lap, I look around the room.

"This space is cozy."

"Like our loft back home, but the view of the ocean is better than the streets of New York."

"I agree, but someday we might have this view or another view." I sit up next to him. "We could move out of the city if you want?"

"The loft is great. Besides, it's spacious enough to raise all our young ones."

I lean against the back of the sofa. "How many?"

"Maybe two, four, or a dozen."

"A dozen?"

"Yes, my love, so we better get started."

He pulls me on top of him, kissing me.

"How about we start with one more, then revisit this conversation after our little girl is born?" I suggest.

"A girl. She'll have your green eyes I hope."

"And your smile."

"Well if she or he comes out like Ben, we will be blessed once again."

I snuggle up to him. "We will."

*

The next morning, I'm awakened by him trailing a flower over my belly, which tickles and lands my knee next to his cheek. I apologize over and over as I suggest a nice hot shower to take away any lingering discomfort. Best decision of the morning. We end up eating on the deck while waiting for our adventure to begin. He pulls my braid, resting his hand on my shoulder.

"How long have you been riding?" he asks.

"Back home I had a picture of my mom on a horse with me strapped to her front. I didn't start riding by myself until I was four. It came naturally to me and when I got my horse Sam, I had my own escape, a new friend, and more responsibilities. What about you?"

"When I was eight. We had stables, I had a trainer, and it was another way to keep me busy without causing problems."

"Did you like it?"

"I did, especially when I took off away from the trainer and hit the jumps full speed."

"You got in trouble a lot, didn't you?"

"I've had my share. Let's hope Ben only inherited a little bit of that behavior."

*

"Excuse me Mr. Tucker, your horses have arrived."

I jump up, excited to have this experience with my husband and to be back on a horse after such a long time.

"You have everything you requested. Is there anything else?"

"No, I think we're good," Michael answers.

He takes my hand and we go out to meet our horses. One is white and the other is brown. Both are very impressive animals. The owner stands with both reins as we make our way out to her. Michael reaches her first.

"Hi, I'm Michael, and this is my wife, Jamie."

"I'm Ms. Abrams. This is Rose and Cricket."

I walk up to Rose running my hands over her body.

"They're beautiful horses."

"Thank you. They're gentle but will give you a full run if you want. When you're done just bring them back here. I am told you are both experienced riders, so enjoy."

With that, she leaves her beautiful animals in our care. Michael puts lunch on his horse and I take the blanket. We start off with a slow walk, then are off to a trot. This is my first time riding a horse on the beach, so I'm looking forward to it. We take a few pictures and find a couple of trails along with an open field to really let them go.

The trails lead us back to a sweet little spot to water the horses while we eat our lunch. He ties them off while I set up our feast on the blanket. Maggie packed sandwiches, a container of fresh vegetables, and fruit filled cookies along with lemonade.

Michael is deep in thought looking out towards the water.

"Penny for your thoughts."

"I love how you make simple things like horseback riding exciting. I used to rush through things, taking it all for granted, but you don't."

I look out towards the ocean, then back to him. "I didn't have a lot of things available to me. Especially nothing like this place."

"Did you ever go to the beach as a child?"

"No. My water experience was our pond. We didn't take vacations because my father worked most of the time. But he always found a way to give me opportunities of fun and learning. I mean, how many people have seen the inside of a silo or seen wild horses where they actually live? I've had baby chickens, goats, and raised two calves with Susan for a school project."

"So, can I spoil you with many destination surprises in our future?"

"I will never say no to spending time away with you." I lean over and kiss him.

"I want Ben to smile like you do when you speak of your childhood."

"He will, because we will give him those memorable experiences. He'll discover and find his way, but we'll be there for him. I hope someday he finds a person to love that will steal his heart, leaving him breathless."

"Is that what I did?"

"Yes." I lean next to him. "You protected my heart first, then you were my friend, and from that we built trust between us. That kind of love is what I hope for our son."

"I'm looking forward to experiencing the future with you."

"It's whatever we want. Right now, I want to be chased." I jump up, grabbing the container of cookies. "Dessert awaits you, but you have to catch me first." I begin to step away and he rises slowly. I clutch the container close when he lunges at me and then run as fast as I can down the beach. I look over my shoulder just as he catches me with one swoop of his arm, pulling my body tight against his.

"I caught you, so what about my dessert?"

Opening the container of cookies, I pull one out. "Do you mean this dessert?"

The container is taken from me then dropped to the sand. "No, you."

After our exhilarating ride on two magnificent horses as well as our chase on the beach, we are now back at our cottage with another end to a perfect day. Inside, Michael checks his phone, realizing we missed a call from his mom. I check my phone and see two missed calls as well. We both look at each other as I dial her number.

"Laura, is everything okay?"

In parent mode, we wait on edge for her to speak. I put the phone on speaker.

"He's fine now. Last night he was crying a little more than normal so this morning I called his pediatrician. He has an ear infection, but they gave him an antibiotic. She said this was the first time he ever had a medication, so I wanted to check in, so you know. She told me it was pretty mild, but to keep an eye on him."

"Mom, did he do okay with it?" Michael asks anxiously.

"Yes. He is asleep right now."

I smile, trying to reassure Michael a breakdown isn't imminent.

"Now you two get back to your honeymoon and I will call you if anything changes. Jamie, try not to worry, sweetheart," Laura says.

"Hug and kiss him for us. Thank you, Laura."

I disconnect the call.

"I know what you're thinking," Michael says.

"It's his first illness. Just mom guilt."

"If he wasn't alright, we would be leaving to go home. You know, that right?"

"I do."

He rubs my arms. "How about a shower?"

I smell my shirt then realize how much one is needed. Michael feels the same as I do about not being there for Ben, but he is in loving hands.

*

The next morning, I wake before Michael and go in search of juice, then check my phone for any updates on Ben. Laura sent a picture of him in the high chair with his face covered in bananas with the caption, "All good." I return to the bedroom with two glasses, finding Michael still asleep. I open one of the shutters taking in the warmth of the sun.

"Why are you not in bed with me?"

"I needed juice. I brought one for you." I hand the glass to him.

He pulls back the sheet. "Join me."

Holding my glass, I crawl into bed beside him and pull out my phone.

"I received a picture of Ben; he's doing better."

"Bananas, huh?"

"Yes, his favorite."

"Did you sleep much?"

"A little bit. You?"

"I won't lie, I felt helpless being here and not able to comfort him even though she has more experience than I do."

"I understand." He smiles. "What would you like to do today?"

"Eat crab, drink beer, and just relax."

"All of that can be arranged. I'll give Roger a call. But first, I have a surprise for you."

"Michael, you have given me so many surprises in the past few days, what else could there be?"

He gets out of bed disappearing in the closet and comes out with an envelope. "Open it."

I open the envelope and pull out a piece of paper that has my family name across it like a logo.

"I don't understand. 'Carson's'—what does this mean?"

"Do you like how it's done?"

"Yes, I do. But what is it for?"

"It's going to be the name of the new bar in New York."

"Why?"

"The meeting I had that day to see the space for a bar is what brought me back to you. New York will be the place that you saved me."

I reach over, touching his arm feeling the same. "Are you sure?"

"Your past is what made you into the person you are today. I never knew I could have someone like you in my life."

"You could have any woman you want, so what do you mean?"

"I never experienced feelings for anyone like I did for you. Your stories of being back home in Texas made me want that kind of future with you. You care and love so deeply for the people around you. You give more than you ever take for yourself. I'm alive inside once again because of you. Carson's is my tribute to the woman I love."

My arms circle his neck and I kiss him. "I love it! I'm honored you want to use it."

"Good, because I'm hoping to get help with the finishing touches inside from my wife's point of view."

"Whatever you need."

*

Sunscreen applied and beers opened, we continue our day, talking about our new business venture. My work at the galleries will continue, so we agree the input I give for Carson's will have to be part-time for now.

Our feast of seafood involved crab legs, tuna bites with a delicious dill sauce, and a green salad. We take a walk along the water's edge and watch clouds move in for the first time since we arrived. A light sprinkle sends us inside the cabana until we hear thunder sending us back to the protective coverage of our cottage. Drying off and changing into dry clothes, I suggest tequila shots.

We rummage through the kitchen finding glasses, limes, and tequila then head back into the living room in front of the open doors to listen to the weather happening outside. The rain is falling outside but inside, we're good.

"Michael, when is your next trip to 42?"

"Probably in the next month. Pete said he's having some personnel issues that he wanted to talk to me about and there seems to be a possible kitchen redo in the future."

"Still having a problem with the sink?"

"That and the floors. We need to meet with a contractor."

"He seemed okay at the wedding."

"Yeah he did."

"If it works with my schedule, I think that Ben and I should go with you."

"Are you sure?"

"No, but seeing Pete made me realize how much I miss him. Plus, I'll be able to meet Eli before he gets too big."

I pour us another shot handing him a glass. "Here's to us, Aunt Jamie and Uncle Michael."

The liquid slides down my throat as I shake my head picking up a lime.

"Are you alright?" Michael asks.

I nod with my eyes closed and get an idea. "Let's go to that bar we read about."

"The Oasis?"

"Yes."

He stands up in front of me. "Race you to the bedroom." He leaps over the sofa as I yell after him.

"No fair! You have those long legs."

I take off after him and he grabs me when I run through the door to the bedroom. I let out a scream of excitement as he covers my mouth, quieting me with kisses and igniting a fire inside both of us.

Chapter 18

Jamie

n hour later we arrive at the Oasis. I chose a blue striped romper with flat sandals, pulling my hair up in a messy knot. He picked out shorts and a pullover shirt.

Over the next few hours we meet two other honeymoon couples and some locals who introduce us to the Oasis Octopus. It's a drink with eight ingredients, four of them being alcohol. Those drinks go down smoothly, but now I'm buzzing, feeling heat in my cheeks and a desire to touch everything under my husband's clothes.

The song changes to a slow one and we find ourselves dancing close as my feelings become stronger and I start to look at him like he is fresh water in a salty ocean.

He lifts my chin up. "We have a problem."

His words have me focusing on his lips, trying to concentrate on what's coming next. My expression changes to concern.

"What's wrong?"

He pulls me closer to him, and I grin.

"I'm not able to drive, and neither are you."

"That is a problem. What about Roger?"

He smiles, touching my lips with his finger. "His number is on my phone."

I jam my hand into his pocket, retrieving the phone. "Here you go."

"In a hurry?"

I run my hand up under the front of his shirt. "Yes."

He dials, then speaks with Roger, sliding it back in his pocket. "He'll be here in ten minutes. Let's settle our tab."

In the back of Roger's car, we act like newlyweds, laughing with our hands all over each other. We pull up to the cottage getting out of the car. I lean down to say goodnight.

"Thank you, Roger, for saving us."

"You are welcome Mrs. Tucker."

Michael joins me. "Roger, how about you take tomorrow off? We have everything we need. Let Maggie know that we are going to be fending for ourselves all day."

"Are you sure Mr. Tucker?"

"Yes. Just see to what we talked about if you would."

"No problem. Have a good night."

We wave goodbye, then turn to go inside.

"What task does he have to do for you?" I ask, curious.

"A surprise for my lovely wife."

"This whole honeymoon has been one big surprise—there's more?"

He opens the door ushering me in, then locking it behind him. "Would you like a water?"

I kick off my shoes. "Yes, I would. I'm going to change out of my clothes. Will you excuse me?"

"Of course. I'll meet you outside."

In search of something sexy in the closet, I grab what I think might just be the element that will send him over the edge. I slip a white V-neck shirt over my head. It slides over my skin showing off my new tan. The hem rests slightly above my waist, leaving a tiny bit of exposed skin before my lace boy shorts cover the rest of me. I let down my hair and shake it free, looking forward to feeling the high my husband causes in me.

He is right where he said he would be, but without the shirt. The moon casts a slight glow across his shoulders. Michael has always had a physically fit body, but during the time we spent apart, he turned it into an even more muscular physique. One that I find hard not to touch.

Moving closer to him, I promise until the last breath I breathe he will never endure that kind of pain again. I know what it's like to feel it every day you wake up until you lay your head down at night. Falling asleep for even a few hours only brought momentary relief but ended just as quick a few hours later.

I run my arms around his waist, kissing his back. His arm comes around and with his hand on my hip, pulls me next to him.

"I was wondering what was keeping you." He turns to take in my pick of clothing. "You are forgiven."

"Were you upset with me?"

"Only because I wanted you here with me. You do know what a white t-shirt does to me."

"I do."

He lifts me up as I wrap my legs around him. "Let me show you."

*

The next morning finds us welcoming the sun through our opened window with a wonderful tropical breeze and a slight hangover. I roll over on my stomach, propping myself up on my elbows.

"I can't believe our time is almost over."

"This place is perfect."

He touches my hair, flipping the ends through his fingers. "How are you feeling?"

"A slight headache, but other than that I'm good. I think food might help."

"I need a big breakfast if I'm going to keep up with your sexual appetite."

"My appetite?"

I get up and crawl on top of him trying to tickle him, but all I get is a broad white smile, a fast flip, and now I'm the one being tickled. I can't breathe, I'm laughing so hard, and he stops.

"Did you hear that?"

"What?"

His phone goes off with a text. He grabs it, reading that Maggie is outside the cottage with food.

"I asked Roger to call her. Let me go see what's up."

I crawl out from under him. "No, I'll go."

He snickers.

"What's so funny?"

He grabs a shirt off the chair, handing it to me and I realize I'm naked.

"You rattle me. That would have been embarrassing." I slip it over my head and pull on shorts. "I'll be right back."

I return a few minutes later holding a platter of fresh fruit along with two plates of eggs to find him dressed in trunks. When he looks at me, I place a strawberry between my lips, sucking out the juice before biting it.

"Hmm, lucky strawberry."

"Let me share so you don't get jealous." I pull one off the tray, putting it in his mouth.

"Roger told her we had been to the Oasis and were feeling pretty good when we returned last night. This egg dish is a family fix to deal with a hangover."

He looks over the dishes. "I'm game."

*

I swing my leg over the side of the hammock, with my sunglasses on to help filter out the brightness from the sun. The egg dish was phenomenal, full of veggies, cheese, and pork.

"I feel better, you?"

He crawls onto the hammock with me. "I feel ready."

"Ready for what?"

"The day, you, and more of you."

"I want more of you too, but what is the surprise for today?"

"Kayaking, fishing, and then dinner at Pinta Point. Which is why we didn't need any help today." He looks out into the water. "That is our charter boat for today. We'll take the jet skis out to meet them."

I crawl out of the hammock to view the boat. "What about the kayaks?"

"When we return. After we eat lunch, we'll drive to Windy Oaks and go out there."

"Sounds like fun. Let me change into my suit, then I'll be ready."

"Or I can help you into your suit, because this t-shirt looks difficult to remove."

I begin to back away from him. "Does it now?"

*

Our charter boat has three on board besides us: the captain, a first mate, and Chuck. He's in charge of assisting with bait, lines, and has many stories to tell us. I'm about to have my first experience catching a large fish and the excitement is pounding its way out of my chest. Michael is watching me, but then his line takes off and now he's fighting alone as everyone's attention is all on me, to make sure I don't get pulled out of the boat.

My struggle ends in a large fish breaking my line, leaving me exhausted and them reassuring me how well I fought for it. Michael's adventure went on for another 20 minutes with him pulling up a beautiful fish now wiggling in the net that Chuck is holding. I snapped pictures of Michael with his Giant Trevally.

We try again, catching two smaller fish along with a shark. My arms are sore, and I hope it doesn't keep me from our kayaking trip later. Michael is used to this kind of upper arm workout, but my arms are feeling the burn. Chuck assures me some ice and a few beers will have me ready for my next adventure.

We're dropped off to board our jet skis in search of lunch, waving goodbye to an excellent crew and great fishing. Back at the cottage, we head to the fridge to find ham sandwiches and a couple of side dishes along with peach tea. We perch ourselves on the beach, enjoying our feast and reminiscing about our fishing trip. Our donation of fish to the food bank in town rounds out our wonderful experience.

A short siesta later we're ready to embark on our kayak excursion. After a quick lesson from the owner and operator of Windy Oaks, Kent, and with our life jackets in place, we set out with our map.

The curve of the shoreline leads us to various coves, giving us views we wouldn't have if we weren't in the water. I corner myself once and Michael's detailed directions of how to get out are magnificently explained and we're on our way immediately. We encounter a family of turtles sitting on a log and watch sailboats out in the water with different colored sails. The weather could not have been more agreeable today, but after three hours of exploration it's time to head back.

Our dinner reservation is at 8:00 so I take advantage of a soak in the tub while Michael opts for a swim. My head rests on a bath pillow when the water suddenly moves around me. Startled, I open my eyes to find him standing next to the tub. His trunks are wet, so I know he hasn't showered yet.

"How was your swim?"

"Invigorating." He bends down next to me. "How is your soak?"

"Relaxing. Want to join me?"

In a matter of seconds, he peels off the wet trunks and is half in and half out of the water when he stops, getting back out. He takes off through the cottage naked and I hear him in the kitchen. I wonder what he's doing when he appears back in the bathroom with a bottle of champagne.

"Would you like a glass?"

"Yes."

He pops the cork letting the overflow fall in the tub. The cold liquid on my leg makes me jump and I splash water towards him as bubbles land on his leg. I giggle, and he steps into the tub, pouring while he sits down.

"You're talented in everything you do," I tell him. "Balancing a champagne bottle, glasses, and getting in a tub, not to mention our successful day of fishing and kayaking."

"How are your arms?"

"Fine." I reach for my glass when I feel his legs on each side of mine.

"I could fit in one of my magic massages before dinner."

"Well I won't turn down that offer."

He sets down his glass then turns me, so my back is against his front and takes my free arm, running his fingers up and down while gently squeezing, along with long strokes down my whole arm.

"That feels so good."

"We had this done for us after a long day of rowing."

I lean back against him while he begins to work on the next arm, taking short breaks to drink champagne.

"Babe, I want to surprise you tonight, will you wait in the living room while I get ready?"

"You've piqued my curiosity, but yes, I will." He kisses the top of my head and lays my arm across my belly. "Better?"

"So much better."

We enjoy our tub time with more champagne along with a lot of relaxation. He gets out of the tub and I watch him brush his teeth, comb his hair, and apply cologne. He turns to blow me a kiss and leaves the bathroom for me to get ready next.

Savannah sent three choices of dinner dresses in case we went out. The dress I choose is a mini strapless bandage style cocktail dress in green. It only leaves me enough room to wear one small article of clothing underneath.

I tint my lips, straighten my hair, then pull on nude ankle strap heels. She sent a small nighttime purse to go with all three dresses, and with one more look in the mirror I'm ready and make my way out to him.

"I'm ready. Sorry I took so long."

"Don't apologize. Jamie, you're stunning."

"Thank you. It's real tight. In fact, I didn't have much room to put on anything else underneath except for something that resembles floss for underwear."

He almost chokes on his water. "Maybe you should show me?"

"I will later, if I'm still wearing it."

I walk past him, grabbing his shirt and pulling him away from thoughts of my tiny article of clothing hidden beneath the dress.

This time we call for a car to take us and bring us back just in case we partake in more drinking. We arrive at the restaurant, which is located on the side of a mountain, giving us views of the water that are breathtaking as the sun begins to go down. He gives the hostess our name, ushering me in front of him.

We place our order for coconut shrimp, fresh veggies, and mashed potatoes. We're drinking our water when the waitress comes back with a bread basket. I look around the room noticing a couple in the corner, holding hands across the table.

"What do you think their story is?"

Michael turns to see them. "That's easy. They're college sweethearts married for 40 years, celebrating today. She's an editor for a magazine, and he's head of a law firm."

"A celebration they take every year, just the two of them. They are very much in love."

"Look, they're going to kiss."

We both look at each other feeling their love. He nods to another couple in the corner.

"What about them?"

"Married on their honeymoon. We met them yesterday."

He looks at them again. "You're right. They're from Florida, in their 30's, with two kids, both hers. He lost his wife two years ago to his neighbor."

"But now they have a second chance at love."

He turns his attention back to me. "An incurable romantic."

"I'm so in love with you that I want this feeling for everyone."

"Tomorrow is our last full day. What should we do?"

"Nothing."

"Are you anxious to get back?"

"Yes, to see Ben, but I've loved every minute of our honeymoon. I miss him, but I'm very happy to have his dad all to myself. The picture of him this morning was adorable with his wagon."

"One day he'll be filling it with toys and frogs."

"Did you ever bring snakes into your home?"

"Once. Then I was grounded for one week, so in turn, I flooded the downstairs bathroom while attempting to send my toy sailors off to sea."

"How old were you?"

"Five."

"I wish I could have seen you then."

"My mother must love me because she had to deal with a lot."

"There is no question that she loves you."

"Just like we love Ben."

Over the next two hours we eat and share a decadent dessert of chocolate lava cake. We call the car service and return to the cottage to enjoy the rest of our evening. He steps just past me after I enter.

"Jamie, wait here, just for a minute."

"Sure."

He comes back out of the bedroom and holds out his hand for me to take.

"I want you to know that romance will always be in our relationship, and if I ever start taking you for granted, you have my permission to hit me over the head with a bat."

"You're always romantic. What's this about?"

He covers my eyes with his hand as I'm led into the bedroom. When I open them, I see flowers, with candles casting a warm glow around the room. I look at him, saying nothing, just reaching to hold his hand.

"I called Roger and he called Maggie, so she followed my suggestions. I wanted a special ending to another perfect day. And to show you how much I love you and that romance will never fail us."

He has no idea what all this means to me. But it's the words he says, and the look in his eyes that speak louder than anything.

"I know what we have together. We'll be the couple in the restaurant tonight celebrating our 50th anniversary kissing and holding hands at the table. I know who you are and who I am with you. The only thing we will have a problem with is when our kids are older and how much we'll embarrass them with our PDA. Now can you help me out of this dress?"

"My pleasure."

Chapter 19

Jamie

ur flight was delayed so our arrival at home was 11:30 pm. We knew Ben would be asleep, giving us more time to wait before seeing our son.

Stepping inside the apartment, we weren't sure if his parents were asleep. Laura wasn't visible, but Harrison was on his phone. Seeing us, he motions for us to enter quietly, pointing down on the sofa. As we get closer, we see Laura sitting on the sofa with Ben fast asleep in her arms. Michael comes around the end of the sofa, taking Ben, and stirring his mother awake. She smiles up at him, placing a kiss on Ben's head. Laura stretches as Harrison tells her that she got caught spoiling her grandson.

"If falling asleep is spoiling, then I think we're okay."

I leave a kiss on Ben's arm as Michael walks down the hall to his room.

"I'm sorry we woke you," I tell Laura.

She stands. "It's fine, we tried to stay awake. You're so tan." She hugs me. "He was a little hyped up because Harrison thought it was a good idea to share a sugar cookie with him."

Harrison comes over to me. "It was just a little bit. Don't let her fool you—she's in love with that boy and takes every opportunity to snuggle. How is my new daughter in-law?"

"I'm wonderful. We could never thank you both enough for making it possible for us to have such a wonderful honeymoon. You being here with Ben alleviated a lot of concern for us."

Michael returns to the living room.

"He's out cold, never woke up." He heads over to his mom giving her a hug, then to his dad. "I know Jamie has already thanked you both, but that resort was phenomenal. All the excursions, the staff, and the weather were perfect."

His dad speaks up. "He's fun. Other than the ear infection, he's eaten well, played, and found a new favorite toy."

"The wagon?"

"Yes, just like his father."

"You remember."

"Yes, I do." They both share a smile of a fond memory from their past.

We sit and have coffee as they fill us in on their time with Ben and we tell them a little about our paradise. Harrison tells Michael about the bar's progress and I share my enthusiasm about the name. After about an hour they decide to go back to their apartment and we turn in ourselves.

The next morning, we're greeted with a bouncy boy with quite an appetite. As I feed him, Michael showers and dresses for work. When he's done, we switch, as he dresses Ben, and I shower. We meet back in the living room just before the nanny is to arrive. I straighten my wrap dress, wishing I was back in my bikini.

"Why are we working today?"

He takes me into his arms. "I could only negotiate a small amount of time away for you."

"I'll miss having you at my fingertips."

"I know. I guess clothes aren't an option anymore."

I look up at him. "Only in our loft."

"How about lunch?"

"Sounds good. Your place or mine?"

"Carson's is our place, remember?"

"I do. I'm excited to see the sign in place."

"Well then you come to the bar and I'll have lunch ready for us."

"Deal."

A small crash interrupts us and we realize Ben has tossed his sippy cup off the tray.

*

Back at the gallery I look down at my phone, walking up the hall to the front desk, and am met with cheers from everyone. After many congratulations, Alysse and I head to my office.

"Jamie, tell me it was heaven."

"Yes, and very private. My tan has never been more even."

"I can only imagine. How were the excursions or did you bypass all of them?"

"We went horseback riding, kayaking, and fishing. There was a beautiful waterfall surrounded by so many colorful flowers. We ate, took naps, and got lost in each other."

I feel my cheeks light up with the warmth of the memories of us back on the beach in our cabana the last day.

"Look at you. Are you blushing? Because if you are, maybe you want to share that story?"

"No, that one I will keep to myself. Fill me in, what am I looking at today?"

"Everything is listed except for the unexpected meeting with Liza. She tried but couldn't find another day to be here this week. Then the videos, 114A, 115A, and 116A. I've updated you on sales from the last four shows like you asked, and they're right there in those folders. Oh, and the damaged art pieces were sent from ELLE, Inc., they're expecting the replacement piece by Thursday."

"Did we find out what happened?"

"No. Mrs. Shepperd only wants to speak with you."

"Gotcha. Thank you again for all the assistance you gave to Michael."

"Were you really surprised?"

"Um, yeah. No clue. But I loved it all."

"Good. Let me leave you to all of this and I'll bring some tea back, Mrs. Tucker."

"Sounds good."

She shuts my door, leaving me to a mountain of work when a white box to my right catches my eye. I walk over to it seeing a tag that says, "Mrs. Tucker." I open it to find inside a frame with a picture of Michael, Ben, and myself at the wedding. I read the note.

"To my beautiful wife on our wedding day, I love you! Michael."

I smile and pick up my phone to call him.

*

The next two weeks fly by as we get a nice routine going on with Ben and the new nanny, along with working out our schedules to have dinner together as a family almost nightly.

Michael is tending to final details and permits and training the staff which keeps him very busy. I decide to walk down to Carson's today to see him after my 1:00 appointment. I walk into a bustle of activity and some of the art I had ordered being placed on the wall as I instructed. My husband is sitting at the oak bar immersed in papers with a plate full of food in front of him barely touched. Time for an intervention.

"Not hungry, I see."

He looks up, smiling at me, but I see the strain of the long days beginning to show in his eyes. His hair shows signs of distress, as he runs his fingers through it out of frustration at this final push.

"I'm hungry now."

I reach past him to grab his plate and bottle of water, brushing his arm with my body.

"Let's go to your office."

He gathers the remaining items on the bar and follows me. We pass two waitresses—one I recognize, the other I don't. She's the one I need to introduce myself to because she seems to be smiling a little too eagerly at my husband and her blouse needs to have a few buttons buttoned. I tuck the bottle under my arm, reaching my hand out to her.

"I don't think we've met. I'm Mrs. Tucker."

She stands straighter as my eyes fell to the front of her shirt. She reaches out her hand.

"Dena. I'm new to Carson's."

"Welcome Dena." I look at Ally standing next to her. "I hope Ally is teaching you well. She's at the top of what she does here at Carson's. She knows we run a family business with lots of Tuckers involved with the business daily. My husband works very hard, but I'm just a few blocks away if you should need anything."

She's smiling, but I knew meeting me today was not on her agenda. I turn to let Michael go in first, as I look back at her. I smile again, then shut the door behind me. I set the plate and bottle on the desk.

"Was that okay? I didn't overstep, did I?"

"No, you were great. You're part owner here and you let her know what we expect from our employees."

"Did you see her blouse and that lipstick? Really?"

"I've been tied up with this permit application today and haven't paid much attention to anyone, until you walked in."

I put my arms around his neck, pulling him into a kiss and melt away his tension of the day. I feel his hands on my back slide lower, resting on my bottom.

"How did you know I needed to see you?"

"You've been preoccupied, and your eyes look like they need a good night's sleep. So, I'm here to take care of you."

He moves in with his lips against my neck. "Come sit with me."

He takes my hand, leading me to his desk chair and pulling me onto his lap, running his hand over my thigh. He pushes my skirt up and as much as I want this encounter to continue, I need to bargain first.

"Michael."

"Hmm?"

"You need to eat."

"But you're better for me."

"I need you well. Please, if I share it, will you eat?"

He stops his pursuit of kissing to look at me. "You win. You stay right here on my lap, and we can eat together."

"Deal." I pick up half the sandwich handing it to him. "Bite, please. The sandwich."

With a new enthusiasm he takes a large bite and nods for me to take mine. As I nibble a bite from the sandwich, his hand slips under my skirt and I let out a squeal. He covers my mouth with his, keeping me from squirming away, then grins.

"I like this game. I will take another bite, please."

"You're quick to learn this game has perks."

"All I need is inspiration from my beautiful wife."

"You could have woken me up when you came in last night, so I could inspire you in a more suitable place."

"I wanted to, but you were sleeping so peacefully. I've been busy more than usual lately."

I hold up the sandwich and have him take a bite.

"I promise it will end soon. Did you see the art being put up?"

He takes the bottle of water, drinking down half of it. On the inside I'm smiling because I got him to eat and drink, but on the outside, he still has dark circles.

"I did, it all looks nice." I pick up the potato salad to spoon him some, but he puts up his hand.

"Switch."

"Switch?"

He's taking advantage of me wanting him to eat, so I comply with his demands. I stand up, pulling my skirt up, so I can sit on his desk pulling him between my opened knees, resting my heels on his chair. His arms rest on my thighs.

"Better?" Before he can answer I pull him by his shirt to kiss him. "Now will you eat?"

"Definitely." He takes in a spoonful of potato salad, chewing it with the precision of a cat about to pounce on a mouse. I pick up the rest of the sandwich as he polishes it off in one bite followed by more water.

"It's hard to resist you when you're being this cute."

I can feel the material of his shirt brush the inside of my thighs as he thrusts his chair forward. "Should we have dessert?"

I run my fingers through his hair. "How about you come home by 6:30, we spend time with our son, eat dinner, and then we can have dessert anyway you want it."

"I'll be home by six."

"Sounds like a plan. Now you have one more bite."

I scoop up the potato salad, placing the full spoon in his mouth. He leans his head into my chest, and nuzzles his nose against the fabric, popping the button open on my blouse.

"You smell good."

I tilt his face to look at me. "Thank you for eating your lunch, but I need to go back to work."

He pushes back his chair, helping me off the desk. I put my clothing back in order. I can walk to the gallery with a good feeling of knowing he ate. I bend to kiss him.

"I love you."

"I love you too. Before you go, check out our bathroom. It's finished."

I move over to look at the addition to the office. "The marble is original? How did it clean up so well?"

"I called the company Robert suggested that worked on the loft apartments. They took care of all the marble and were able to clean the tile in the bathrooms. No replacements needed. Look in the cabinet."

I open the door to find a small bag. Taking it out, I find all my favorite products inside.

"Do you plan for me to come by more often?"

"Yes, I do."

There's a knock on his door. He now has that look, again.

"I guess I've kept you in here too long."

Going to the door, he opens it to reveal Daniel, his manager.

"I'm sorry to bother you, but the beer rep is here."

I step over to the door. "Hey Daniel, no problem, we just finished lunch."

Michael is looking at me, but answers him. "I'll be right out."

I can see the tension settle in his shoulders and his fingers run through his hair again.

"I could stay if you need me to?" I suggest.

He pulls me over to him. "If you stay, I won't make it out there to see the beer rep."

"Okay but I'll see you early tonight, right?"

"It's a promise."

"Let me help you. I know how tough you are, but I'm right here. Use me."

His eyes light up as his eyebrow raises. "That's tempting."

*

He comes home at 5:45, changing his clothes, then changing Ben's diaper, and setting him in his walker before joining me in the kitchen.

His hands rest on my hips and he squeezes. "What's for dinner?"

"Enchiladas."

"That sounds delicious. What can I do?"

I grab a beer from the fridge, pop the top, and hand it to him.

"You can go play with Ben, I'm almost done other than putting it in the oven."

He pulls Ben around in his wagon and they disappear for about ten minutes. When they return, the wagon does not, but they have an arm full of stuffed animals.

"We're setting up a zoo. Would you like to join us?"

"I would."

We sat on the floor for the next 25 minutes while the enchiladas bake. We make animal sounds and set up exhibits until the timer goes off for our dinner. We proceed to sit at the table and begin to eat.

Michael is cutting up vegetables for Ben, when I sit down with them.

"Do you have to go back out?"

"No, I'm here with the both of you all night."

"I don't want you to think you can't be at the bar doing what you need to do. I'm just concerned about you."

"I know. We've talked about what kind of dad I want to be, and I need to be sure it happens. Besides, I've left my new bride alone a lot lately."

"What you're doing is important to our family. We're still learning to balance it all. We are newlyweds, new parents, and business owners. That's a lot of responsibility, but we got this."

He takes my hand and presses it to his mouth.

"That's what I realized after you left today. The long days, bringing work home and not putting this little guy to bed or giving him a bath—it's not what I want. I talked with Daniel about taking on more responsibility and he was all for it. If I need to, I will hire a second manager." He reaches over, touching Ben's head. "My family is too important to me. So next time you see me going too far, pull me back to you."

"I remember you speaking of a bat once."

"I prefer what you did today, but I did say that."

"Well you are all mine for tonight, so I have a little something planned."

He looks at Ben. "Hey little buddy, I need for you to sleep through the night tonight. Deal?"

He picks up Ben's little hand as they high five.

When dinner and dishes are done, I go back to check on my two boys, finding both sitting in the rocker with a book about frogs. Ben sees his bottle in my hand and begins waving his hands and kicking his feet, making funny little noises.

"Do you want to feed him while I go tend to a few things?"

"I think he's going to handle this himself. When did he start holding his own bottle?"

"A few days ago."

I see disappointment on his face. "Remember we can't catch everything he does."

He smiles. "I know."

"Okay I'll go but I'll be back to check on you guys."

I'm in the bathroom lighting some candles when he walks in.

"Babe, this looks great."

"Welcome to your evening of relaxation. I want this handsome face of yours to loosen up. Come to me."

"Are you sure you're going for relaxation?"

He walks over and I reach for his shirt to pull it off. I begin to take down his sweatpants when I notice he's not wearing briefs. I look up at him.

"Your cheeks are red."

"I'm sure they are, please get into the tub."

"Are you joining me?"

"You don't want to soak in there by yourself for a while?"

"Please join me."

"I'm going to check in on Ben, then I'll be right back."

When I return, he's in the tub laid back with his arms draped over the sides, head back and eyes shut. I set down the monitor and begin to take off my clothes to join him.

"How's the water?"

"It's good."

He extends a hand to help me in. I sit down, pulling my hair into a twist.

"Just think of this tub and my body as therapy for the rest of the night."

"May I schedule more sessions, because I don't think all of my issues will be handled tonight."

"I'll send you my contact info."

I pick up the sponge and begin to run it over his skin. We talk, relax, then don't relax, finding many enjoyable ways to release tension. As I look at him sprawled out over the bed sleeping, I feel relieved that I'm able to get him right where he needed to be. After checking in on Ben, I join him in our bed leaning over to kiss his forehead.

He whispers a sleepy, "I love you."

"I love you. Now go to sleep."

He pulls me in next to him with one arm draped around me. Snug in his arms has got to be the best place on earth to be.

Chapter 20

Jamie

The opening night for Carson's is finally here. I leave work early to settle Ben with the sitter and am now at the bar for whatever needs to be done. At 42 bar I wasn't allowed to handle alcohol, but tonight as a partner I'm ready to get my hands into all aspects of operation.

I look around for my husband and see him behind the bar. Our partnership is more on him right now, since I'm still full time at the Gallery. As such, I've taken on more of a role in taking care of him, rather than being physically here day to day.

"Excuse me, sir," I say playfully.

He looks up from the beer cooler. "I'm glad you're here."

I go around to meet him and he slides an arm around me, placing his other hand on my cheek and giving me a kiss.

"What can I do for you?"

"Be my eyes."

"Anything you want. I'm proud of you, everything looks amazing!"

He kisses me again. "We create wonderful things together."

"This is true. I'm off to the kitchen while you work your magic out here."

In ten minutes, the doors will open to the New York crowd waiting outside for our soft opening. Michael speaks words of encouragement to the staff, thanking them for all their hard work.

Taking my hand in his, he gives permission for Daniel to open the doors. The turnout is more than we could have ever imagined. We're met by our friends who have brought along people they know, as well as new customers whom we hope will become regulars.

We're celebrating our new bar, but there are other groups of people celebrating their own events—a couple of bachelor and bachelorette parties, three birthdays, and a retirement. As the evening progresses, we discover our weaknesses, and fix a refrigeration issue.

"He has you working tonight, huh?"

"Max!" I hug him. "Why didn't you call us?"

"I like an element of surprise. You look fantastic. Where is your old man?"

"If you're speaking of my hot husband, he's over there. He's going to be so happy to see you. Where is Maci?"

"Nursing a sprained ankle. She gives her well wishes for a successful opening."

"Isn't she due to have a baby soon?"

"Any day actually. I'm flying back tonight."

"Max?" Michael has spotted him. "What the hell man, why didn't you let us know?" He comes over, grabbing Max's hand in a shake/half hug.

"I wanted the WOW factor. You look good for an old married man."

"Dude, you're three months older than I am."

Max looks at me, then at Michael. "Why do you have her working tonight?"

Michael slides his arm around my shoulders. "Partners in life. How about a drink?"

"Bourbon shots for the three of us. Jamie, you're in, right?"

"Yes, let's celebrate!"

"Now that this bar is open, where's the next one?"

"I think we'll stop for a while and lay roots right here. Jamie's job is still growing and with the other two bars we're good for now. We're going to Hopson soon, and then I want to take her to see the one in Colorado."

"Back to Hopson? Jamie, how do you feel about that?"

"I'll have Michael and Ben, so it will be fine. I have to remember the good things that happened there, not just the bad."

Max holds up his glass and we do the same. "Here's to the strongest couple I know."

I smile at him and look at Michael.

"I mean it," he says seriously. "What you both went through could have pulled you apart, but you're stronger and in a better place."

We clink our glasses. I can't help but think about what he just said. There were lots of times when I was apart from Michael that I feared that when I did make it back to him, he wouldn't understand the reason for our separation the same way I did. But our hearts were tied together by magic and a promise of forever.

*

It's already July with hot temperatures outside sucking up everyone's energy and leaving us to seek out cooler temperatures inside whenever possible. We attend a few baseball games with Ben and go to the zoo and the park on most Sundays. We've been to the beach, and sometimes drive out of town for a little out of the city therapy.

I go to see my gynecologist for a checkup to be sure I'm doing all I can for a healthy pregnancy, if it happens. Our son is now seven months old and we would like to have a new little Tucker in the family.

Michael is busy with the bar here and working remotely for the other two bars. His birthday is coming up, so I've planned a trip to the beach with his parents and Ben as well as lunch. Then they'll take the baby home with them while we enjoy a night out at Trezza Hotel where we got married. I set up a couple's massage, purchased gifts, and am now waiting for his special day to arrive. I missed his birthday last year, but this year I'm planning to make it up to him.

Alysse and I have met with a new client to inventory her collection. We decide to treat ourselves to a little shopping on the way back to work. I want something out of the ordinary for our night away, so we go into Amelia's.

As I'm flipping through the racks of lace, satin, and straps, Alysse brings over a leather combo which leaves my eyes big as saucers and her giggling at my expense.

"Over the top?"

"A little bit."

She goes to put the ensemble back when I hear a customer speaking to the cashier. She's complaining about the heat and how it's impacting her vacation in the city. I glance up at her and freeze, staring at her. Just then, a nearby employee drops some boxes on the floor, causing everyone to look my way. There's no time to hide, but I turn away from her and see Alysse coming back to where I stand, holding more clothing options. I stare at her unable to form words.

"Jamie, what is it?"

I divert my eyes towards the counter when I hear my name.

"Jamie? Jamie Morgan, is that you? Oh shit, you're alive."

My hands clutch at the items I'm holding as I turn to face her.

"Lola."

She looks at me, clearly wondering if it's truly me. "Jamie, what happened to you? Does Michael know where you are? Does anyone know you're alive?"

My mouth opens but I don't want to reveal that he does. "I'm sorry, but I need to go."

I drop the items on a table near me trying to stay calm as I make a mad dash out the door onto the sidewalk, not looking back. Alysse catches up with me, grabbing my elbow and out of breath.

"Jamie, slow down. Who was that?"

"She knows Stacey. They knew each other back at Hopson."

"What?"

"Did she come outside?"

"I can't tell—wait, the store clerk is ushering her back inside," Alysse says. "You're shaking. Come on, I know where we need to go."

Panic has set in with different scenarios playing out in my mind. Does she still know Stacey? Are they still friends? Will she call someone letting Stacey know I'm in New York? We stop in front of Carson's. I take in a deep breath trying to calm down before entering. I see Daniel and ask if Michael is in and he sends me to his office. Alysse never lets go of my arm.

Michael is coming out with his laptop when he sees us and realizes something is wrong. He sets down his laptop and addresses us.

"What's wrong?"

"Jamie, I'll be at the bar."

I nod and Michael takes me inside his office shutting the door behind us. Then I'm in his arms releasing the tears that I've held since seeing Lola and trying to calm my breathing. His arms hold me tight, but my brain isn't talking to my body, telling it to calm down.

"Jamie, what happened? Are you hurt, is it Ben?" He pulls away, touching my face with his thumb. "Babe, talk to me."

I focus on his face and steady my breathing. I lay my forehead on his chest, resting my hands on his hips.

"Ben is fine. I saw Lola."

"Who?"

"Lola. Stacey's friend from Hopson. The redhead with the freckles."

"Where did you see her?"

"At Amelia's. She asked what happened to me and did you know. She couldn't believe I was alive. I ran out without Alysse and down the sidewalk when Alysse caught up with me. What if she speaks to Stacey? I'm so tired of this, I want it all to go away. I feel stronger until something like this happens and then I fall apart. What is wrong with me?"

"What you went through was traumatic. I know seeing her brings all of that back. I wish I could take it all away for you—it kills me that you are still suffering."

"I don't, not all of the time. You help me stay in the present and like I say, most of the time I feel strong. It's just that Lola has the power to change our lives and that scares me."

He lets go and walks over to his desk. "You're right. It scares me too."

"It does?"

"Yes. Now knowing everything you went through and having you and Ben in my life, I think of what can go wrong all the time. I need to be on guard but I also want to give us the life we deserve. It's not easy and I get what you're feeling—you carried this alone for so long."

"All I wanted to do today was buy sexy lingerie to wear for your birthday."

His eyes narrow as his beautiful smile appears. "We can find another store so you can follow through with your plan?"

A giggle escapes me.

"We have a long way to go, but we will figure it out. I can walk you back to the gallery if you'd like."

"No, I'll be alright."

"Are you sure?"

"No, but I need to be."

A few reassuring kisses later we both enter the main bar. Alysse is talking with Daniel but cuts off when she sees us.

"Everything okay?"

"It is now."

"Ready to go?"

I look at Michael. "I'll see you at home later."

"Call me if you need me."

With a kiss and hug he walks us to the door. I stay busy the rest of the day working on a photography showing that's coming up in a couple of weeks. The young artist division of Robert Shaw Galleries is developing just as we hoped, with expansion imminent.

*

Upon my arrival home, I'm informed of Ben's day, shown cute footprint art which I hang on the fridge, and change my clothes and his diaper. Now he's enjoying a juice and crackers.

When he's done, we get back on the floor to enjoy block building while watching the cutest program on baby animals at the zoo, one of his favorites. Every time they bring out a baby giraffe, he finds it in his pile of plush toys bringing it to me.

I watch him with such love in my heart. He is the reason I need to stay strong, but he is also the reason I still hang on to fear. When the show is over, I put him in his walker in the home office and go through the mail. I see an envelope from Caleb and ask Ben, "What do you think it is?" His response is to drool over a teether he has his hands on.

Inside is a note.

Hope to see you guys soon, before Eli goes to preschool! I've sent pictures and a gift for Ben. Call me this Saturday and we can video chat. We love you! Caleb.

I flip through the pictures seeing one of Eli destroying a cupcake, one of him sleeping peacefully in his car themed bed, and one on his father's shoulders. I smile, knowing he is better without Stacey and that Caleb has moved joyfully into being a father.

Laying the photos down on my desk, I go over to my son. "You two little guys are why I need to keep myself in a good place." I pick up a toy and hand it back to him. "What do you say little man, is it time to visit Hopson?"

He hands me the toy and puts his hands up. I pick him up, spinning him through the air, out the office, and onto the floor while I make dinner. When Michael arrives, we eat then plan on going to the theatre near us for a movie where Ben takes a bottle and sleeps through the whole show.

On the way back, I bring up Hopson. We both agree it's time.

*

Thursday proves to be busier than usual probably because I want to leave early for Michael's birthday celebration. My goal is to leave by 10:30 to meet his parents at the beach.

Alysse rings in, letting me know that my appointment has arrived and is downstairs waiting for me in the exhibit room. He asked to see the collection we had currently running to see how it compared to his. I didn't see the harm since George was working in there, so I gave my okay. I grab my computer and head downstairs, looking over at Alysse who is covering Tanner's break.

"Don't get comfortable at the front desk, I need you up with me."

She giggles. "But I get the first view of everyone who enters."

I smile, not knowing what I would do without her in my division or as a friend. Entering the exhibition room, I pass George who is leaving to get more tools. I search for my next appointment, who I find standing in front of the biggest piece of the collection.

"Mr. Stewart?"

He turns to face me. His hair is messy like he just rolled out of bed wearing worn jeans, a t-shirt, and sneakers. I hold out my hand to greet him as he takes off his sunglasses looking me over from head to toe. I look down in response, wondering if I have something all over my dress.

"Well aren't you a vision." He reaches out, grabbing my hand with both of his. "It's a pleasure to meet you. Your voice on the phone matches you perfectly."

"What do you mean?"

"Sexy."

He did *not* just say that. "Shall we get started with the interview?" I ask, ignoring his comment.

I walk past him as he follows me to the window. He steps up close, a little too close for my liking.

"What is that intoxicating smell?" he asks. "You smell like summer."

My voice now has more authority as I feel he's overstepping in a big way. "Mr. Stewart, how can Shaw Galleries help you?"

He steps away, spinning around on his heels to face me. "That's an open question because I can think of a few things you can do for me."

My brow wrinkles as anger settles. "May I ask why you wanted to meet me today? Because all you have done so far is make me uncomfortable. I'm not flattered at all by you or your comments and frankly I think you are older than the clients we're here to help."

He puts his hands up under his chin and begins to apologize. "I'm sorry, Ms..."

"*Mrs.* Tucker," I emphasize.

"I'm sorry if I am attracted to you, but you have what I like in a woman." He pulls out his phone and snaps my picture.

"What are you doing?"

"Looking for my perfect match. I'm getting good vibes from you—like we could create magic together. Do you feel this chemistry between us?"

I step away from him. "No, and I think what you are looking for is not Shaw Galleries."

"Aw, come on. You have my number, how about you give me yours? One I can call late at night when I feel inspired."

"ALYSSE!" I call out loud enough that he shakes his head slightly but keeps grinning at me.

She comes into the room. "Is everything okay?"

"Call George. He needs to escort Mr. Stewart out of the gallery."

She looks at us and I shake my head for her to do as I ask, leaving me alone with him again while she finds George.

"Hey, wait a minute. I'm just playing with you. I would love to be represented by Shaw Galleries, especially if it includes you." He reaches for my hand and I move away from him as George reenters the room with Alysse.

"George, please see that Mr. Stewart finds the door."

As George reaches for him, he pulls away.

"Take it easy, big boy. I changed my mind. I don't think Shaw Galleries can help me, but we can still make magic happen, Jamie. This gallery rocks with beautiful women."

"Get out now. Or I will call the police and have them make magic with you."

He walks past Alysse and winks. George follows him to be sure he leaves.

"Jamie, maybe we need better screenings," Alysse suggests.

"He was creepy. I don't think he was here for art."

"Odd guy—a little older than our normal artist."

"Artist or not, he needed to go."

After that disconcerting appointment, it's time for me to meet my family, so I gather my things, and then text Michael to see if he's ready. He responds yes, and I tell him I will be there to pick him up in 15 minutes.

I've already touched base with his parents to meet us at our designated spot and called to make a few adjustments to the hotel room for tonight. I slip into a casual halter dress and a pair of flat sandals. Today, we celebrate the wonderful man who is my husband.

Chapter 21

Jamie

ichael is standing outside of Carson's, looking good in his summer attire. His arms struggle against the shirt as he slides his hand into his front pocket looking at his phone. I whistle and he looks up at me.

"My wife has come to save me."

I give him a kiss first and foremost. "Happy birthday, handsome."

"Thank you."

"Are you ready for the beach?"

"I am."

"The car will be here in seven minutes. Tough day?"

"Why do you ask?"

"You're clenching your teeth which makes your jaw twitch. Sexy, but concerning."

"Sorry. How was your day?"

I don't want to tell him about my overeager client from earlier, so I just give a simple answer.

"Okay, but it's better now."

I hold him close, keeping his mind on me and not his day when our car arrives.

*

The beach lifts our spirits as our baby boy is amazed with sand, water, and a puppy not far away from us. Michael's parents take a stroll down the beach as we play with Ben.

"Ben, do you think we can talk Mommy into a puppy?" Michael looks up at me with the sweetest eyes as Ben crawls onto my lap.

I kiss the top of his head, rubbing his tiny feet as he squirms babbling and pointing. I glance at my husband who is now eating chips.

"You can talk me into most anything, but a puppy?"

"Can I now?"

He moves over, kissing my exposed leg, and moving my dress hem up even further.

"We have this little one and adding a puppy that pees on the floor and needs walking…maybe we should think about it when we get a house."

"Are you thinking about a house?"

"At the moment I'm thinking about you kissing my leg, but I think having a yard for Ben and a grill sitting on a deck with a small vegetable garden would go great with a new puppy."

"I agree."

He stands and takes Ben down to the water as I pack up our basket. I join them to kick around in the water until it's time for us to leave.

With Ben settled in his car seat, I kiss him repeatedly making him giggle. I give him a bottle knowing he'll be asleep before they get into the city. Michael says goodbye to his little champ and speaks with his father while his mom and I sit in the airconditioned vehicle with the baby.

I look over at the two men. "Laura, do you think they're speaking about something serious?"

She peeks up over the seat where she's belted in by Ben.

"Yes, but don't let it ruin your night out. I want the two of you to enjoy the city and have a nice night at Trezza."

They walk back to the car and Harrison opens the door for me to get out. "Laura, are you good? Is he asleep?"

"Almost."

Harrison leans over and kisses my cheek as Michael walks around to say goodbye to his mother.

"Thanks again, Mom," I hear him say.

"You're welcome. Now go have fun with your wife. Happy birthday, I love you."

She hugs him as Harrison gets inside the car and we watch as they pull off with our son.

"Are you going to tell me what that serious conversation was about?"

He slides an arm around my shoulders. "No worries tonight, it's my birthday. That was nice having lunch on the beach. Thank you."

"I'll wait until you're ready to talk, but right now you are all mine. Let's go play video games."

"Awesome."

"Maybe skeeball, and that water race with the horses."

"We can do them all."

*

Our leisurely walk through China Town leaves our bellies content, and a few sakes later we head to our hotel destination. I pull my phone out to call our car.

"It will be here in five minutes."

"You're cute trying to keep your secret, but do I get a hint as to what comes next?"

"No, but later I'm going for hot sultry vixen."

The look on his face is exactly as I expect. "Okay, did I pique your curiosity?"

"Heck yeah."

"Good, because our car is here."

We get into Artie's car, sit back and enjoy our ride to Trezza Hotel which is slower than usual, due to traffic issues. The car stops in front of the hotel and he looks out to see the entrance where he stood the night of our wedding.

"We're staying here?"

"Yes."

We thank Artie who wishes Michael a happy birthday, before stepping out onto the sidewalk.

"This is good. I never would have expected this."

"Good, I surprised you. We're having a couple's massage, drinks, and I have a couple of gifts for you."

"I'm not sure about the massage."

"You'll love it; besides I'll be on the table next to you."

We arrive on our floor and as I try to put the key into the door, he's kissing my shoulders, leaving a trail across my skin. The nerves all over my body are on high alert and I wiggle.

"Babe, I can't get the key…"

He spins me to face him, kissing the thoughts right out of my head and making me concentrate on the feel of his lips taking over mine. He moves a hand up in my hair, pressing my lips closer to his. In a smooth move, he has the key in the door and us inside before I realize, and me against the door.

"Did I help?"

I stop, getting my bearings when I realize we are indeed inside the room. I exhale.

"Helpful, and might I add, great kissing."

"We could pass over the massage and I could tear you out of this dress and have my way with you."

"But we need this material between us for now, because people will be here in 20 minutes for our massage. While we're waiting though, I have a gift for you from Ben."

I pull him over to the sofa. On the table is a wrapped box.

"Open it."

He tears off the paper and opens it. Once he sees what's inside, he looks at me clearly surprised.

"How did you get this?"

"At the last game we went to with Ben, you spoke so much about seeing your favorite team that I made some calls. Every player signed it."

He holds the ball. "This is awesome." He kisses me. "Thank you, babe."

"Keep looking inside the box."

He pulls out a piece of paper to reveal the second part of his gift. "Season tickets, box seats?"

"Yes. You can take whoever you want at any time."

He cups my face. "Thank you."

Looking at my watch I realize what time it is. "Come on birthday boy, we need to get changed."

"Into what?"

"A towel."

*

When our 45-minute massage is over he's relaxed and playful. He has me up against the corner of the sofa before I can even show him my gift. I'm loving his hands moving over my body and his teeth tugging at my ear. I love everything about him.

"Michael, I have one more gift for you."

He stops, sitting up next to me. "I can't wait."

"Will you pop open the beers from the mini fridge? I'll be right back." I kiss him and leave the room to give him what I hope he will love on me. I'll love having it removed by him.

He's talking to me from the other room as I change into my new purchase. I decide to cover it with a white terry robe from the hotel, leaving him to wonder just a little more. I walk out to find him by the window still in his towel.

"Oh, you need a fuzzy robe like this one."

His expression is one of love. I never feel sexier than when the color of his eyes darken, giving me the look that turns me to putty. He smiles, picking up the two bottles and comes towards me.

"So, you are my gift."

I turn up my beer. "Have you had a good birthday?"

"Yes. It's so much better than last year."

I step away from him, pulling at the belt that holds my robe together and take one more draw off my beer before setting it on the table.

"I hope this will be the cherry on top of your wonderful day."

I drop my robe to the floor to reveal a purple lace halter corset with matching bottoms. From the intense look and slight grin from my husband it's a good choice.

He steps over to me touching my waist, circling around to take in my whole look. My eyes are fixed on his mouth, wanting him to kiss me and my teeth pull on my bottom lip. He runs his finger over the laces while his other hand pulls me closer to him.

"Best gift ever."

His smile tells me he loves it. His hands are in my hair holding my neck while his lips tease me with soft, but firm kisses. When I feel his warm breath on my exposed shoulder, a moan escapes me. I press against him feeling his muscles contract. My hands run along his arms keeping me steady and the space between us close. I look up at him.

"I'm all yours, what do you want to do?"

A couple of hours later we're laying across the bed eating vending machine food, drinking ginger ale, and making plans for our Hopson trip. He's lined up small cheese crackers on my back, eating them one by one.

"Are you ready to tell me what's bothering you?"

He takes the last cracker into his mouth, his lips soft on my skin.

"I received a call this morning from Pete's stepdaughter, Lacy. She thinks he's in trouble."

I turn over on my side. "What kind of trouble?"

"When she asks him what's wrong, he snaps at her. He seems to be under stress that makes him forget to do normal everyday things, which we both know is not like him. He's so regimented. She thought if I came in that maybe I could get him to talk to me. I pulled up some reports from the 42 in the computer and noticed some discrepancies."

"You've always been able to talk to him, of course you should go."

"Will you and Ben go back with me?"

"Sure.

"You have to tell me if you start feeling concerned once we arrive. I want to be there for Pete, but I need to know you will be okay."

"Yes, of course I will."

He reaches over and cuts off the lights as I put all our discarded wrappers on my nightstand settling back in beside him.

"I hope you can help him."

"Me too."

*

The clock next to me reads 6:45. We need to get up, shower, and go back to work today, which is hard after our special day and night. In the elevator we're discussing grabbing a bagel from the café down in the lobby when his phone vibrates. He pulls it out of his pocket.

"It's Pete."

"Maybe he's reaching out to you."

He answers. "Pete, what's up?" Then his expression changes. He's talking with someone but it's not Pete.

"When did it happen? How bad? When will you know more? No, no, it's okay. I will be on the next flight out. Thank you for calling."

He begins to punch out a text when we get off the elevator, stepping to the side.

"Michael, what is it?"

"That was Lacy. Pete is in the hospital."

I cover my mouth. "Oh my God. Why?"

"Last night he was at the bar working when he started to exhibit signs of a heart attack, but they think he was poisoned."

"That's crazy."

"The bar has been closed by the police pending an investigation. They won't let anyone in until I get there."

"What is his current condition?"

"Critical."

"I can make some calls to go with you, but I don't want to take Ben. Do you agree?"

He looks up from his phone. "It's probably best if he doesn't go. I'm sorry—this is not what we planned."

I give his arm a light squeeze. "It's okay, Pete needs you."

He leans in for a kiss and takes my hand as we leave the hotel and catch a cab.

*

Back at our loft, we spend some time with Ben while we pack. His parents listen to Michael explain about the previous phone calls to Pete and now this. His old friend is unconscious, in critical condition, and no one knows why.

We're able to get a flight out that afternoon, allowing me to have Alysse come and go over everything that needed attention for the next few days because I don't know when I'll be back. Robert understands how important Pete is to our family and knows I have to go.

When I'm done with my bag, I pick up my son and hug him to me, kissing him and smelling his baby scent one more time. Ben holds his stuffed bear toy and rests his head on my chest, looking up at me with dark eyes like his father. He's tired because we kept him up past his nap time to spend time with him. I smile, loving how he settles in my arms.

Michael comes into the bedroom to finish his packing. He stops and smiles at us. Looking at him I know what's coming next.

"Don't even say it."

"What?"

"You're going to tell me it's okay for me to stay here while you go to Hopson."

"It's true though. I know leaving Ben is hard for you and it's Hopson we're going back to."

"Leaving Ben is hard for you too, but Pete needs us. What if..."

He comes over to us and kisses Ben, taking him out of my arms. "Do you know where my grey sweatshirt is?"

"Yes. What else do you need?"

He shakes his head, not really concentrating on clothes.

"Jamie, who would…I mean, how could it even happen that he was poisoned? It makes no sense."

I begin to pick shirts, slacks, whatever he needs, along with some running clothes. I zip up the bag, but not before grabbing his toiletry bag from the bathroom.

"I think we're ready. Are your parents back yet?"

"No, but do you want something to eat?"

"Yes."

*

When his parents arrive, Laura comes over rubbing Ben's back in his chair.

"Hey sweetie." She touches my arm, stopping me from cleaning off the table. "How is Michael doing?"

"Upset—confused how this could even happen. Pete means so much to him."

"I know. He was like a father to Michael when Harrison wasn't. We owe Pete a lot for helping him. Are you going to be okay going back there?"

"I want to say a confident yes, but I can't. Being with Michael, seeing Pete…it's all I can think about. Thank you again for being here to take Ben. There isn't anything that I can tell you that you don't already know. I'm sure you didn't know how much you both would be involved with him when you moved here."

She hugs me. "Take care of each other. We will take care of Ben anytime you need us. Don't worry."

Michael appears. "Jamie, we need to leave or we'll miss our flight."

He comes over to say bye to Ben, then kisses his mother on her cheek. I do the same, then hug Harrison goodbye. With one look back at them in the kitchen with Ben, I smile. He begins to cry, tearing apart my heart, but I know he is safer here than at Hopson under this cloud of concern.

*

In the car to the airport, Robert calls to speak with me about the odd creepy client yesterday, and me having him removed. I mention he took my picture which I had forgotten about until just now. Michael turns to me, waiting for more information when I end the call. His phone goes off, but he only briefly looks at the number and puts it back in his pocket.

"What happened yesterday?"

"I didn't want to ruin your birthday."

"Jamie."

"I had an odd encounter with a supposed artist who thought making advances and inappropriate comments was a way to get a date, I think. I had him escorted out by George."

"What kind of advances? Did he put his hands on you? What is Robert doing about it or about your safety when you're out with new clients?"

Michael seems to be over-the-top concerned about the incident so now I know something else is really bothering him.

"He's looking into new measures. I might stop on-site evaluations unless I have one of the guys go with me." I look at him. "What else has happened? You seem off."

He sits back and pulls up a text from Brandon, the new assistant manager at 42. He hands it to me.

"I got this an hour ago when I asked if he had seen any changes in Pete or any situation with employees and Pete. That's what he sent to me."

I read over the text.

"None of this sounds like Pete at all. Having an affair with an employee, catching him in compromising positions, and lashing out?"

I hand Michael back his phone only to sit looking out the window not believing anything I've heard today. I lean into his shoulder.

"We will figure this out."

Chapter 22

Jamie

irst stop is the hospital. We don't even drop our bags at the hotel, wanting to check on Pete's condition first. The drive through Hopson from the airport gives me a chance to see places from my past. The strip mall, the store I got my first items for the apartment, and even ECON. The college is further down so I'll see that and the apartment complex when we go to 42.

We stop at the information desk in the emergency room when we hear Lacy calling to us. It's clear the situation has taken a toll on her. She's not the spunky, funny trainer that she was during my first day at 42. Her eyes are red and puffy and she's clutching a tissue in her hand. Michael sets down the bags to console her.

She lets him go of him, blotting her nose with the tissue when she sees me. Her eyes widen as she opens her arms to me. I hug her, wanting to take away her pain.

"Jamie, it's so good to see you." She touches my cheek. "Both of you look so good."

Michael asks her if there is anything new to report.

"Nothing good. They confirmed the suspicion of poison in his system. They're not sure exactly what kind or where it might have come from, but they want to keep the 42 shut down until further notice. His house is also being investigated. You need to speak with the police chief. I told him you were on your way here."

"Thank you."

Michael turns to me. "Jamie, will you be okay while I find him?"

"Yes." I turn to her. "Lacy, how is your mom? This has got to be hard on her."

"Trying to be strong. She's cried so much, but everything that's happened over the past couple of weeks has exhausted her."

"Michael filled me on what he knows. What can I do for you and your family?"

She starts to cry. "Pray for him. It's bad, really bad."

I take her into my arms hoping to give her a little comfort but know it's only a temporary fix.

Michael returns from speaking with the police chief. "We can go in to see him, but only for a few minutes."

*

We enter his room listening to the machines. He's lying in the bed hooked up to monitors as well as a ventilator. He's pale and seems thinner than when we saw him at the wedding.

How does something like this happen to a guy like Pete?

Michael takes my hand as we approach the bed and look at our friend struggling to fight his way back. I reach down taking his hand in mine. I speak to him, and so does Michael. We want him to know that we are here for him. This is hard on Michael to see Pete like this. I slide my arm around his waist.

"He's a strong man, he will be fine."

"I hope he makes a turn soon. We need him to wake up."

We leave him only because we're asked to and join the family in the waiting room. The chief is ready to meet us at 42, so we let Lacy know she can call us at any time.

*

We stand outside the hospital waiting for a car. First stop will be to the 42 to meet with the police chief, then to call the Dean of Students and schedule a meeting with all the employees.

As the car takes us to the bar, we pass the apartments where we met and fell in love. The college adds even more good memories as we pass, but it's hard thinking about the reason why I left.

The 42 looks the same on the outside. A bar should be a fun place to visit, but today it has yellow caution tape across the front and two police officers posted outside. We get out the car with our bags as Michael shows the officer his ID, who also looks at mine and checks his list. We're waved through and proceed inside to meet Chief Johnson.

"Mr. and Mrs. Tucker, thank you for getting here so fast. We have lots of questions and we hope you can shed some light on the situation for us."

"Whatever we can do," Michael answers.

"You have to excuse me, but I'm relatively new to the force. I come from Hampton County. I've been reading over records from the bar complaints and altercations. I found one on you Mrs. Tucker, which leads me to your disappearance about a year ago. It's good to see you are okay."

"Thank you."

"This is an unfortunate situation concerning my department with the safety of everyone involved. Mr. Tucker, I would like to escort you to the office upstairs if that is alright?"

"Yes." Michael looks at me for confirmation.

"Go, I'll be right here," I say.

I look around the bar with all the police officers and forensic personnel and stand right where I am, not wanting to interrupt their investigation. The stage is the same as I remember when Michael would sing while playing his guitar. I love to hear him sing to Ben. There's the dance floor where I surprised him with a New Year's Eve kiss. The area where I had my fight with Stacey before our trip to Colorado. I close my eyes trying to forget the bad and be in the present.

Chief Johnson comes back down to find me standing in the same spot. "I'm sorry, these guys should have given you a chair. We're done with the investigation of the office upstairs. You can join your husband."

"Thank you." I reach the office door and peek around the corner, finding Michael behind the desk looking over a ledger. "Hey."

"We can leave after I gather some information to take with us. They released the files and the computer."

I walk over to the desk to find a picture of Ben and me. He notices.

"I sent it to Pete. He acted like a proud grandpa."

"That's sweet."

"Would you call the employees and let them know to meet us at the hotel tomorrow night at seven?"

"Sure."

We sit for two hours making calls to employees and looking over files, making a list of people to call tomorrow. When hunger pains made his stomach growl, he realizes how long it's been since we ate and has our luggage sent over to the hotel with one of the officers.

"Let's go eat. How about Taco Hut?"

"Sounds good."

*

At Taco Hut, we see a few students and a team dressed in workout clothes from practice.

He wipes salsa off my lip. "They used to be us. It wasn't that long ago."

"No, it wasn't. Now look at us. Married with a child. The 42 looks the same."

"I haven't authorized any changes since I left. It holds memories of you, of us, and I didn't want it to change. I kept the apartment, but I'm ready to let it go. I texted Caleb. He wants to see you."

"I thought about it, but it depends."

"On what?"

"If you need me."

"I always need you, but tomorrow I'm meeting with the Dean, so that might be a good time to go see him and Eli, then I can come pick you up."

"Okay. It will be nice to see them."

*

We arrive at our hotel in a taco haze. I call Caleb and set up our visit while Michael texts Lacy for changes on Pete. There aren't any, so we call home to FaceTime his parents, but Ben is sleeping. Laura says they tired him out at the train exhibit. I knew they had gone because of the pictures she sent me earlier of him and Harrison sitting in a train car. Michael takes the phone, filling his dad in about everything we know so far. When all the phone calls are done, we both lean our heads back on the sofa.

Then I stand up, holding out my hands. "You're tired and so am I. Let's go to bed."

He picks up his head, almost forcing his eyes to open as he reaches for my hand. "Sounds good."

After brushing our teeth, washing off my makeup, and pulling on a t-shirt, I climb into bed with him. He shuts off the light and holds up his arm for me to snuggle up against him.

"Jamie. I know being here in Hopson is difficult for you."

"Hey, this is where I want to be."

"I love you."

I smile at him before snuggling back down in his arm, laying my head against him. "I love you too."

*

The next morning, we go to the hospital after breakfast to check in on Pete's progress. After that, it's over to the 42 and before his meeting with the dean, Michael drops me off at Caleb's parents' house.

"The last time I saw you was on your wedding," Caleb says by way of greeting.

A smile appears on my face as I walk into his outstretched arms. "Hey you."

"Mrs. Tucker, how are you?"

"Under the circumstances, I'm okay. What's up with the beard?"

"What can I say? The ladies love it!"

"I'm one of those ladies. It makes you look…"

"Sexy, mysterious?"

"Manly."

"Well considering who your husband is, I'll take it. Come on in."

The house looks the same except now there are toys, baby gates, and loads of pictures.

"Where's Eli?"

"He's asleep, but due up any minute. My parents are at work. It's just you and me."

He puts his arm around my shoulders, walking me out onto the patio. I sit down at the table while he pours tea into our glasses. There is a plate of cookies on the table which he hands to me.

"I know you like my mom's chocolate chip cookies. But I also bought lemon bars."

"Yum to both." I look around his large backyard with my mind on Michael.

"How is he taking all of this? I mean, it doesn't seem real."

"He's worried about Pete who is still unconscious. We saw him, he looks so frail."

"How are you?"

"A little uneasy. You haven't seen her at all?"

"No. Like I said at the wedding, once she signed the papers of custody over to me, she left and hasn't been seen. Jamie, you're safe here."

The baby monitor lights up with the sound of a young child.

"He's awake!" I say.

"I told him you were coming. I will be right back."

Caleb leaves to get Eli. Over the monitor I can hear him talking in the sweetest voice. He changes Eli's diaper, explaining that Aunt Jamie is downstairs. My heart aches for many reasons.

Eli turns up a sippy cup as they come outside. He looks just like his pictures and video chats, but in person, he is real stinking cute. Caleb lowers Eli to the patio and his son hooks his arm around his leg.

"He's really not shy. How about you sit on the blanket over there where his   toys   are."

"Okay." I follow his suggestions and within minutes Eli is handing me toys and feeding me crackers. I wipe tears off my face. Caleb looks at me, tapping my leg.

"Too much?"

"No, he's amazing. Caleb, you're a daddy."

"I never dreamed I would be a father at this time in my life, but he fits. We get each other. His life and happiness all come first now. I wouldn't change it. I owe Michael so much. He helped me find out about her pregnancy, but he's the one who secured a lawyer for the paternity test. We love Uncle Michael, don't we Eli?"

Eli claps his little hands and squeals, going over to climb into his truck which he pushes with his feet.

"What's going on with you?" What are your plans?"

"Well this being my last year at Hopson, I'm bouncing around some offers. I might be accepting a job in Redon. My Aunt Mary lives there and has offered to keep Eli when I'm at work. She has a small rental two doors down that I can use."

"Anyone special?"

"No. But I'll keep looking. Eli helps me by pulling ladies to us."

I reach over, smacking his arm. "That's how you use your son."

"Come on, I'm sure when Michael is out with Ben alone, he attracts lots of women."

"Not what a wife wants to hear. But yes, he draws a lot of looks from the ladies even with me. Ones at work, at restaurants, and on the sidewalk. He has one of those faces."

"Maybe the ripped body has something to do with it, too?" Caleb suggests. We both laugh.

"I know he only has eyes for me, but I still have a little green monster waiting inside of me if she needs to come out."

"You have no reason to ever worry. No man could love a woman more than he loves you."

"Thank you for that."

"Jamie. I have to ask," Caleb starts. "If Eli looked more like Stacey, would it be hard for you to be around him?"

"No. He's an innocent child and luckily he has you."

Eli brings me books to read, then crawls into my lap. I'm melting from his sweetness.

"See, you attract all kinds of guys," Caleb jokes.

I cut my eyes at him. I sway back and forth while sitting with Eli and see Caleb watching us. "My heart has been filled by another wonderful little person. I promise to always be here for him."

We spend the next hour playing with Eli, taking him out to his swing, then filling cups with sand from the sand box. Caleb takes me upstairs to see the nursery decorated in Hopson colors. We pause to change Eli's diaper, then go back outside.

We're reminiscing about our time at Hopson when the doorbell rings.

Caleb stands. "It's probably Michael. I'll be right back."

Eli stays with me while Caleb gets the door, and then returns with my husband, talking about the placement of this past year's rowing team. He stops when he sees me with Eli.

I smile up at him, Eli sitting in my lap. I turn my head up to greet him with a kiss and then he sits down beside us.

Michael picks up a truck, diverting Eli's attention. He crawls off my lap over to the truck. Michael holds his hand up for a high five which Eli matches. Then he asks for a hug, which Eli gives. Michael hugs him, then rolls across the floor with him, tossing Eli into the air. The child squeals with laughter then says, "Again."

Michael sits back up with the toddler hanging over his shoulder, whipping him around for a tickle attack.

"Did you guys have a good visit?" he asks.

"We did. How was the meeting with the Dean?"

Caleb rolls a ball to Eli, who climbs off Michael to retrieve it.

"It went well. I told him I would be back in touch when I learned more, but the 42 will stay closed until the police release it."

Caleb stands to pour another glass of tea. "What about footage inside the 42?"

"They're going over it now. What are you feeding this kid?"

"Everything. Not a picky eater at all."

"I see you've been working out."

"I'm trying to be like you."

Michael hurls the ball at Caleb's head. I watch them interact. Their relationship is different, closer.

"Is there a bromance happening here? Should I be concerned?"

"We reached another level of friendship, yes."

Caleb hurls the ball back at Michael. "We went through a lot before Eli was born."

"Yep. I have a brother now."

I look at Caleb then back at my husband. "That's so sweet."

Caleb takes my hand. "I'm glad you're back with us."

I fight back tears, those words making me realize what the past year has put us all through.

*

Out by the car we hug each other, knowing our lives will forever be tied together in a way we never imagined when we met our freshman year. Little hands push their way between us, but when we separate, Eli hugs me with one arm and Caleb with the other. Michael takes a picture with his phone.

Putting it back in his pocket, he says, "Jamie, we need to be going."

"Yes, I guess we should."

Caleb scoops up Eli onto his shoulders. "It was good to see you guys. You'll keep me posted on Pete, right?"

Michael shakes his hand. "We will. Coming to New York soon? Jamie gave me box seats for my birthday, so a baseball game is in our future."

"You guys get back home, and we'll set something up. It will be fun seeing the two boys play together."

I hug Caleb once more, then climb into the car. We wave goodbye and I miss them already.

As we drive back, Michael fills me in on the meeting with the Dean as well as what he wants to cover with the employees at the meeting tonight.

Lacy calls, saying Pete was moved to a more secure room on the 4th floor where he could better be monitored by staff with security. Not knowing how he was poisoned makes security a bigger concern. His condition has improved, but he's still very sick.

Chapter 23

Jamie

e haven't been back to our hotel room since leaving this morning, so I need to respond to emails while Michael calls to check in with Daniel. Then we both get on the phone with his parents to see Ben—after our meeting later, he'll already be in bed.

The conference room in the hotel is set up for us and 42 staff begin to fill the seats. Some faces are familiar, but others are not. I know an explanation is needed about my disappearance, but my biggest concern is Pete.

Michael introduces himself for those who have not yet met him, and then it's my turn. He motions for me to stand and takes my hand in his.

"This is my wife, Jamie Tucker. She once worked at the 42 when we attended Hopson together. For those of you who knew her then, you're aware she went missing for over a year. I won't go into the details, but I'm telling you because unthinkable things happen to good people."

He continues, "Pete is important to our family. We are reaching out to all of you for any information you can share with us that will hopefully lead us to the reason he is in the hospital in critical condition. The doctors detected a substance that had been given to him over time, causing confusion, irritability, even problems with mobility. He collapsed when his body couldn't support him. The 42 seemed to be the place where he could have been receiving the substance, so it will be closed while they investigate."

He turns to me to continue.

"We have contacted the vendors and the Dean. You will be paid in full during this period of closure and I will need everyone to check in with me before leaving tonight to be sure I have your correct information. The 42 is a family atmosphere, so this situation needs to be kept within our family. We are not trying to hide information from anyone on the outside, but we want his family to have the time to work through their personal crisis." I turn back to Michael to let him finish.

"I am asking that you cooperate with the police, but not to speculate—only give them information that you have is true. Now, I want to open the floor up to you guys. Did you see anything? People or deliveries that seemed off? Incidents inside the 42 that I may not be aware of with customers?"

He looks around the room waiting for someone to speak up, but no one does. We decide maybe people will talk in a less structured atmosphere, so we invite everyone to grab a beverage and something to eat while we gather their names.

I tend to the computer while Michael goes around and speaks with them. I meet Ally, Derek, and a girl named Carla who are all new to me. Carla seems young and a little nervous. She keeps looking at me and I wonder if she has something to say, so I finish and go over to her.

"You went through a lot, didn't you?" she bursts out when I reach her.

Maybe she's just curious about my situation.

"I was taken against my will, forced into leaving the people I loved," I answer honestly. "I never knew something like that could happen to me, but it did. Fear drove me away, but I found my way back. Pete is very dear to us, and we need to do everything we can for him. I noticed you've been with us for three months?"

"Yes. I live about 20 minutes out of town. I have five siblings all older than me, but I didn't get their outgoing personalities."

"Why did you apply for a job at the bar then?"

"A listing went up in the bookstore. I'm a sophomore with a few close friends and this was a way I could break out of my shell."

I smile at her. "I get it."

"I've never met Mr. Tucker, but Pete speaks about him a lot."

"They've always been close." I look over and catch Michael's eye, waving him over to us. "Michael, Carla said she has never met you in person—she's only heard about you from Pete."

"It's nice to meet you, Carla. Welcome to 42."

She's at a loss for words and her cheeks say why. I get it. He still does that to me.

"Thank you, sir."

He sits down next to me. "Please call me Michael. What is your job?"

"I bus tables. I'm not sure how I got the job, but Pete has always been nice to me. Kimber came along about the time I did."

"Who?"

"Kimber. She was a waitress, older than me and a lot more confident." She looks down at her hands.

"Carla, is there something else?"

"She seemed to be into Pete. Oh, I'm sorry that was speculating."

"Did you see something specific to make you feel that way?"

"She worked when he did, even helped him in his office. Usually where he was, she was."

"I don't recall her being here tonight."

"She left. We haven't seen her lately."

"Do you know if she left on good terms? Is she a student?" Michael presses.

"No, actually the last time I saw her was four days ago when I took out the trash. She was coming down the steps from the office then went out the back door. I do recall one time walking in on them. Brandon sent me upstairs to give a package to Pete. He was sitting in the chair behind the desk and she was sitting on the desk, kind of leaning on it in front of him. She moved away, smoothing her t-shirt and he seemed embarrassed. I'm not sure what was going on exactly, but I clearly interrupted them."

"We appreciate you talking with us. If you can think of anything else, give us a call." I hand her Michael's card.

"Definitely. Thank you for the opportunity to be a part of 42. It's really a fun place to work. I hope Pete gets better soon."

Michael stands as she walks away. "Maybe we need to find Kimber."

Stuart comes over after she left. Michael thanks him for his help the day Pete passed out.

"No problem, he's a good man. I overheard what Carla was saying. I caught them in the kitchen once. I don't know what it was about her, but he seemed to be interested in her. They were laughing and her hand was on his arm." He switches gears, smiling at me. "Jamie, it's good to have you back."

"Thank you, Stuart."

Meredith smiles and walks over to us, giving us both a big rocking hug. "I've missed you guys. Married life must be good."

I look up at Michael, smiling. "It's very good. Hey, what do you know about Kimber?"

"I heard about her through some of the other waitresses, but I've been out of town. Why?"

Michael speaks up. "It seems Carla and Stuart shed some light on her that makes us want to find and speak with her about her involvement with Pete."

"I have nothing concrete, just rumors."

He touches my arm. "Jamie, I'm going to speak with some of the bartenders before they leave. Meredith, always good to see you."

"Same here."

We let everyone go after informing them about where to pick up their checks. I pack up the computer when Michael answers his phone over by the door. Hanging up, he slides it back into his pocket, walking over to me.

"Lacy called and said Pete opened his eyes briefly but closed them soon after. They're moving him to stable condition."

"That's good, right?"

"We'll take any progress we can get. I guess we need to concentrate on Kimber. Maybe some of the files I gathered today will help us."

"How about we go upstairs and order some dinner?"

"That sounds good."

*

The sofa is calling my name as I choose to leave the adulting on the other side of the door. Michael sits next to me, trying to release the stress that has been building for the past few days. I look over at him feeling hunger pangs before picking up the phone for room service.

"How does a cheeseburger sound?"

"With fries?"

"Of course. I'm going to order a side salad; do you want one?" I crawl across him to reach the phone. His arms lift as he watches me try not to disturb him, but in my mind it's exactly what I wanted to do. When I reach my destination, I feel his hand smooth out my pants, following my legs down and resting on my calves. I place our order, then sit facing him on his lap. His hands move to rest on my hips.

"We have 40 minutes, what would you like to do?"

He leans into me and my body reacts to being this close to him. He kisses me, but I take it further, deepening the kiss. That's when he bumps me off over onto the sofa and stands up. Bending down, he scoops me up and throws me over his shoulder, heading out the living room. I pat his back, starting to pull his shirt out of his slacks.

"I like the view from here. Maybe I need an updated picture."

I hear the smack on my bottom and feel a little burn. He sets me down in the bathroom where I move my hair only to be met with his lips once again on mine. This time he is in control and I love it. He stops.

"We are going to have a race."

"What kind of race?"

"The race is whoever can get out of their clothes first. Ready, set, go!"

I start to scramble with my clothes trying to ask him what the winner wins, when I begin to struggle with the hook on my pants. I'm twisting and jumping, though it's not helping. He, on the other hand, is completely naked before me.

"Not fair, it's stuck."

"Plenty fair. Now I get to watch you undress for me. Remember the clock is ticking for our room service."

I scramble with my pants, but once undone, I slip out of them, then peel off my shirt and bra.

"Well, I guess you won."

"I did, because I got to watch you undress."

"I'd say we both won. Shower?"

For a little while we are honeymooners without a care in the world, washing away our worries and escaping with each purposeful touch and kiss.

Afterwards, I slip on pajama shorts with a t-shirt and he slips on cotton shorts with a t-shirt when we both hear the door at the same time.

We're very excited the food is here since we're now both famished. Michael goes to the door while I put my wet hair up in a knot. We sit on the floor in front of the coffee table to eat.

I let out a long yawn. "What do you think of the things Carla and Stuart said tonight?"

He leans back against the sofa, wiping off his mouth and placing his napkin on the table.

"I don't know what to think. I just need him to wake up, so we can talk. Nothing that I am finding or hearing is Pete. He's not the type to cheat on his wife and at the bar, it's insane."

"I agree. It opens up even more questions."

"Let's talk about you."

"Me?"

"You haven't said much about how you are feeling. Seeing everyone today must have stirred some memories."

"It did, but Pete needs us to be focused on him."

"Jamie, you are my wife, my priority. I don't want you putting all this before yourself."

"My life has so much in it that any bad thoughts I'm having get pushed aside when I see you or think of Ben. It felt good to tell them tonight, to put my leaving in the open. You, my sweet husband, are my beacon to all that is good in my heart."

His eyes soften and he smiles. "I'm here for you, always."

"I know you are."

I lean over to kiss him, knowing we can face whatever comes our way. We sit on the sofa going over papers and checking the employee files when I come across Kimber's file and notice it's not right.

"Michael, there are things in her files that are missing. I know by helping you with Carson's that these files should have the same information."

"What's missing?"

"Her social security number for one. And her address is incomplete." I reach for my phone to look up the address. "I can't find this zip code anywhere near here."

"That's strange." He opens the computer to pull up log sheets that are kept at 42 on new employees, incidents etc. "There is no mention of when her first day was at the bar. Did you find a background check?"

I flip some more. "No. It's like she didn't exist, but we know she did from what they have told us."

He looks away then back at me. "Why don't we go to bed and start fresh in the morning?"

"There's something else," I say, looking at his face. "What are you thinking?"

"That this is overwhelming, confusing, and just plain crazy. We won't solve anything tonight, so let's go watch mindless TV in bed until we fall asleep."

"Okay, no more thinking."

Chapter 24

Jamie

With a sudden foreboding, my eyes pop open as Michael's phone buzzes loudly next to the bed. He picks up and an agitated voice spills out. When calls come at this time of the morning it's usually not good. I sit up, trying to figure out if he is talking to someone here or back home. The person stops, giving him the opportunity to speak.

"Slow down, I don't understand. Is he alright?"

I crawl out of bed as our eyes lock. His close. Whatever has happened has knocked the wind out of him and I'm anxious to find out what as he finishes the call.

"Someone tried to kill Pete."

My mouth is open, hand on my stomach. "Is he okay?"

"Yes. Chief Johnson asked if we could come down to the hospital."

I begin scurrying about the room, picking up jeans, a shirt, and pulling on a hoodie. Michael does the same. I grab my phone and my purse, and slip on shoes, waiting for him in the living room while I put up my hair.

He comes out to join me.

"What happened?" I ask.

"A nurse came in to get his vitals and caught a person covering Pete's face with a pillow. She started screaming out a code to alert others and that's when she was run into by the assailant. Let's go."

*

The hospital is alive at such an early time of the morning. There are extra police cars in front of the entrance, keeping any new people from going inside. The officer at the door recognizes us and sends us to see the chief.

We make our way up to Pete's floor and as the elevator doors open, we are met by more officers. Chief Johnson is speaking with a nurse when he spots us.

"Mr. Tucker, Mrs. Tucker, I'm sorry to have to bring you both down here at this time, but I need to speak with Mr. Tucker if that is okay?"

"Of course."

"Can I see his family?" I ask.

He points past us and I see them sitting in the corner, visibly upset.

Michael turns to me. "Go to them, but please don't go anywhere by yourself." The concern on his face is real.

"Okay."

He hesitates, not wanting to leave me but is called away by Chief Johnson.

I make my way over to the family to try and console them any way I can.

Lacy stands to meet me. "Jamie, I don't understand, why would someone do this?"

"I don't know, but we will find out. Where is your mom?"

"She fainted. They took her to a room, then she woke up frantic. They gave her a shot to calm her down. There is an officer and a nurse with her. Jamie, does Michael have any idea?"

"No, I'm afraid not. He's speaking with Chief Johnson. Maybe after that we'll know something. Pete will pull through this."

She hugs me tighter, crying on my shoulder. I have no words to help her, nothing.

We sit together, awaiting news. Michael returns but his expression is different—he's angry. His eyes are fixated on me. I stand up, waiting for what he's about to say.

"Jamie, I need to speak with you, alone."

I look at Lacy. "Will you be alright?"

"Yes, go."

He takes my hand, moving quickly to a hallway nearby.

"Michael, what's wrong?"

"They have footage of the person who tried to kill Pete. It was a woman."

"Was it Kimber?"

"It was Stacey."

I stare up at him and he gives me time to process his words.

"Why would she try and hurt him?"

"I don't know, other than maybe she thought it would bring us back here. She knows we would do anything for him. We need to leave and go back to the hotel with two undercover police officers. They have set Pete's family up with protection as well. I'm sure she's pissed her attempt was unsuccessful."

His arm circles around me, guiding us out of the hospital. I look over at Lacy who is speaking to the chief and Michael's grip tightens. We are led to a car waiting outside.

*

Back at the hotel I sit down on the sofa as he brings me a bottle of water, then leaves to speak with the officers. After a few minutes he comes back over to me.

"What are you thinking?"

"We need to let Caleb know."

"Chief Johnson sent over a car. I called him from the room when I saw it was her."

"And Ben...what about your parents?"

"I called them from the car. You didn't hear that conversation?"

I take a moment to think, shaking my head and trying to loosen the fog that's monopolizing it. I set my water on the table and get up, walking away from him. When I turn around, he's just watching me. He doesn't know what to do either. I'm sure he is just as dumbfounded by this new revelation as I am.

"What happens next?"

"Confirmation."

"I thought we had that."

"No. I know it's her. But we need concrete evidence."

"She ran out. What kind of evidence could there be other than her picture on the camera?"

"Fingerprints, more footage throughout the hospital."

"Is Chief Johnson coming here?"

"Yes. Once they go over everything. Do you want to try and get some sleep?"

"No. I'm going to shower. Could you order up some breakfast? Maybe some coffee with a shot of bourbon?"

"How about I get us a bottle?"

It takes about 25 minutes of hot water therapy to wake me up from this nightmare. My hair is wet, so I braid it and slip on a pair of jeans with a light blue pullover. I join Michael out in the other room where our food has arrived. He holds up a small glass with brown liquid.

"See if this helps."

I throw it back.

"Do you want to eat?"

"Yes. May I have the next one in some coffee?"

"You got it."

"While you were showering Caleb called. He's worried about you and told me to tell you he loves you. Should I be concerned my brother loves you?"

I touch his arm. "Like a sister."

He shoots me a smile. "I do have some good news. I received a text that the 42 has been released and can be reopened."

"Michael, that's great news. So, does that mean they didn't find anything?"

"The Chief said he would fill us in when he gets here later. Are you feeling better?"

"I feel horrible for Pete's family, I miss my son and I'm angry."

He takes my hand. "I know."

"I also know you are trying to be strong for me." I walk over to the window and look out at the street below. "I didn't do what she wanted me to do, which was disappear out of your life. Do you think Lola told her about seeing me?"

He comes to stand next to me. "It's possible."

"Do you think she's Kimber?"

He runs his fingers through his hair. "Maybe. Which means she saw the picture in the office, maybe heard him on the phone talking with me. Carla saw her in the office, so she probably went through things. It could have been me that made this happen. I brought all of those people to our wedding, what if…"

"No, don't ever think what you did for us caused this to happen. She is a sick person, full of hate and I know she shot Josh. She was going to kill me I have no doubt in my mind. If I had come back to be with you, I feel she would have done something to you or the baby she was carrying because you would have chosen me." I pull him to me. "I can't believe she and I share blood."

"We need to confirm that if we get a chance."

"I agree."

*

My coffee is extra delicious with the bourbon along with the extra shots, but now I've turned to water. I'm feeling the warmth on my cheeks and also a lot less tense. We're sitting on the sofa facing each other, propped in the corners. I'm only sort of reading the magazine from the hotel, as Michael looks over emails. A knock at the door makes me almost jump off the sofa.

He touches my leg. "Hey, you okay?"

I acknowledge hearing him, but I'm not ready to hear the words that she has resurfaced.

Chief Johnson comes into the room in plain clothes. He sees the bottle of bourbon and the two glasses. I stand to greet him.

"Mrs. Tucker."

Michael joins us. "Please sit down."

Chief Johnson is a gentleman in his 40's, tall and slender. He has a gentle smile, but I feel the folder he's carrying is not good news for us.

"I'm sorry to say that your suspicions are right."

He opens the folder, laying pictures on the table in front of us. There's a picture of a woman he calls Kimber, a drugstore photo of the same woman, and then a few from the hospital cameras. Her hair is red and her clothes are basic, not her usual designer outfits. She wears no makeup. Michael picks one up.

"Do you have fingerprints, or anything else that will tie her to Pete?"

"Yes." He pulls out a report on what was found at the 42, then what was found on the door in Pete's room.

"She didn't wear gloves during her attempt?"

"She did, but we brushed everything in that room, and found prints that matched ones found at the 42 up in his office and around the bar. It's obvious she's been in his room before the actual attempt. The woman in the hospital is Stacey/Kimber."

I pick up my glass and pour more in, asking if they want one with me. Both shake their heads no. I down the brown liquid all at once, then exhale. Michael lays his hand on my leg.

"Mr. Tucker, you said Pete knew Stacey from before. How did he not know that Kimber was Stacey?"

"I can't answer that. We'll have to wait till he wakes up."

"I want you both to come down to the station later to go over details to keep you both safe. We need to step up security and I need more information, anything you can give me. We just need to find a way to pull her out, get her to slip up, and find out if anyone is working with her."

He stands, and we follow.

"I will see you both about 4:00 at the station."

Michael extends his hand. "Thank you."

Chief Johnson looks at me, nods then leaves.

Sleeping was not something we were going to be able to do. Michael showers and at 4:00 we're at the station going over details of a plan. What they want us to do is stay inside, away from the public eye, except for normal outings so they can monitor our situation. If she tries anything, then they hope to be there to catch her.

We leave, but my gut tells me there must be a better plan. The two officers, Dixon and Peatus are still with us. They'll escort us in and out of places, hopefully away from danger.

Michael calls the hospital and gets a report on Pete. He's resting comfortably, and it seems his organ function is back to normal. Now it's a waiting game for him to wake up.

We go back to the hotel where we call home to video chat. Ben is crawling on the floor playing with chunky cars and trucks. Hearing our voice on the phone brings him over to Harrison. He sees us and touches the screen with his hands, looking around to try and figure out where we are, causing us all to laugh. He says, "da da" over and over. I begin to play peek a boo with him when he says, "ma ma." The emotion of this whole messed up situation grabs my nerves, twisting them. I now know what I need to do, but I need Michael on board.

*

Our dinner consists of steak, a salad with goat cheese and a glass of wine. When the cart is taken out, I close the door, turn and meet Michael in the middle of the room. Grabbing his hands we lock fingers.

"Can we just be us for a while?"

"How about a movie in bed?"

"Perfect"

A few hours later…

Michael sets his glass down on the table forcefully, spilling the contents.

"No. I won't let you put yourself in any kind of danger. I can't lose you, not again. We'll find another way."

I touch his arms, placing my lips on the back of his shirt. His muscles tense. Gone is the relaxed state we were both in earlier, replaced with the fear from my proposal. I know he wants to say no to what I'm suggesting, but I need him to see it's the only plan that we have.

"Michael, I want to make sure we never feel the pain of losing each other again or having someone we love harmed by her. I feel this is the only way."

He turns to face me and the look he gives me stabs deep. I know he's not mad at me, but he's mad that we might have to do this to be able to end it. He walks past me to the window.

"No."

My voice wavers. "Please, you have to agree with me."

His shoulders fall, and he places his hands on the windowsill. "You can see the reflection of the moon in the lake from here." He hangs his head. "When I woke up from the accident, no one believed me when I said I saw you with Josh until they searched the vehicle for fingerprints. I had no idea if you were…"

"Dead?" I whisper.

"Desperation overtook me as I searched for you. The only thing that numbed the pain of missing you was alcohol. I felt alone for the first time since meeting you. The one person who fit in my life perfectly had vanished. About five months into your disappearance, I left the 42 after drinking one night. It was late, and the campus was full of college students. As I wandered around not wanting to go back to the apartment alone, I came upon a group of girls who were leaving a party. They weren't feeling any pain either and one took a liking to me. I thought maybe I could let go of the stabbing feeling I carried with me every day, but she didn't kiss like you; her hands didn't move across my skin touching me the way you did. We were in her room, and she was into me, but all I could see was you and those green eyes. She pulled off my shirt, so I thought, okay this is going to happen. But she put her hand up next to mine and I realized her hand didn't fit mine like yours. My head spun as I sat back against the wall. I grabbed my shirt and left.

As the days passed, I was up and down. I tried to keep Pete's words in my head to fight, stay positive, but the struggle inside of me was too much. I would lay in bed at night not sleeping for hours and when I did, my dreams would be of you. Hope failed me some days, but I fought to keep going, to find out what happened to you. Seeing your coffee mug in the cabinet or those green kitchen towels I bought when you moved in always took me back to the love I've had for you, which kept me moving forward."

He finally turns to me. My arms are wrapped around myself and tears fall down my face. My sleeve is wet from wiping them off.

"When I did find you, I vowed never to let you go, to keep you safe, to make you mine forever. That is what we are supposed to have together, our forever. But what you are proposing could take you away from me, away from Ben."

My heart sinks deep in my chest, but I have to fight for this. "I knew leaving you would hurt you—it wasn't what I wanted to do. But I saw no other way then, and now this is the only way we will ever be free. She hurt us before, but now we are stronger together. She tried to kill Pete, twice. I'm ready to fight for Ben, for my life back, and for you. I won't let her continue tearing us apart. I remember those days without you which is why we need to do this."

He looks down at the floor, but I want his eyes on me. I've never seen him this upset, clenching his jaw, his body tight. He's struggling and once again it's my fault. He walks to the coffee table and flips through the pictures.

"Jamie, there was no doubt when I saw the hospital footage that it's her."

I take a step towards him but stop. "This will work, it has to. I want more with you, to travel and have a normal life with a house full of family and friends. I received pictures yesterday with information on Susan's Vegas wedding."

My voice doesn't sound confident about my plan, but I take a deep breath. "I don't want to fight with you."

Before I can speak another word or plead with him, he's standing in front of me, my face cradled in his hands and his thumbs stroking my skin.

"If we do this, we do this together. You stay with me the whole time."

"I will."

In my eyes he sees the fear that stays within me and I see pain in his, caused by the person we need to stop. This has to work.

Chapter 25

Jamie

I'm in need of coffee. Coming out the bathroom and slipping on a sweater over my night shirt, I see Michael is still asleep. We stayed up late last night devising our plan to present to Chief Johnson today. I call room service to order food and coffee, then send a text to Laura. It will be a few hours before she responds, so I set my phone down and stretch, walking back to the bedroom.

"You're awake."

He stretches. "Good morning, how long have you been up?"

I sit down beside him. "Not long. I guess we had our first fight."

"Not a fight, but we made up like we did."

A smile crosses his lips when I tell him food and coffee was coming.

"We can do this."

"I still feel we shouldn't, but I understand."

After eating bagels with cream cheese and drinking two cups of coffee, it's time to get dressed to see Chief Johnson.

I choose a grey fitted dress and black heels, wanting to look confident with a little hint of sexy. I'm smoothing out the fabric when Michael comes in the room whistling. I turn to him with my hand on my hip.

"Do I look confident and sexy?"

"Yes, yes, and definitely yes!"

"Good." I walk over to straighten his tie. "You look good."

"Sexy?"

"Definitely yes." We both look in the floor length mirror.

He takes my hand in his. "We got this."

*

Our first stop is the hospital. Pete is still making good progress, so a little of the heavy weight is lifted off all of us.

We call the employees to have them meet us at the 42 later so we can fill them in on what's about to happen. Michael calls the Dean, informing him of the opening as well. We also call a cleaning company to come in and clean the whole place and others to help change the setup in the bar to suit our plans.

Chief Johnson is not totally sold on the plan, but he leaves the details up to us, filling in with help from his staff. We stop at Dot's for lunch, then walk to the bar for our meeting.

Our plan is to be visible. We want her to see we're together, happy, and making this bad situation into a good one, despite her attempts to destroy our lives once again. The risk is that we don't know how she'll attack next. I promise to stay close to Michael and I don't want to give him a reason to regret agreeing to the plan.

I watch him as well. He's consumed with keeping me safe, while watching out around us without seeming to be. We want to show PDA everywhere we go, which comes easily.

We wait for everyone to arrive and when they do, they seem concerned. After the details are gone over, they're all onboard. They split up and get everything done. We buy pizza for the staff's dinner and about 10:00 pm, the last employee leaves.

Meredith comes back before we lock the door. "I put out all the flyers. The place looks good, more open. You guys are sure about this, right?"

Michael runs his hands through his hair, turning away from us. "Why are you asking?"

"Because if she is going to attack, well...this is just crazy."

"Yes, it is," Michael agrees, looking at me. "But Jamie and I agree it could be the fastest way to bring her out in the open."

"Guys, that's dangerous."

"It's all we have. Meredith, please don't say anything to anyone."

She sighs. "I love you both, but please be careful."

We look at each other, heeding her words.

*

The hotel room gives us some sense of security. Everything that we did today, we will repeat tomorrow, but with the bar open.

Holding a glass of wine and looking out the window, I'm lost in my thoughts until I feel his hand on my back.

"What are you thinking about?"

"My dad wanted me to find my sister and now I wish I had never gone back home to see the lawyer. I wouldn't have that information for her to steal, she wouldn't have faked sleeping with you, or been able to claim the baby as yours, and we would never have lost our time together. Some people say you should forgive and forget. Forgiving people was never hard for me before, but I feel no forgiveness towards her, only regret. What's wrong with me?"

"Don't let her take away what you know is in your heart."

"She's evil. How can she be a part of my father?"

"Stacey picked her path. What she has turned into is someone who I want to disappear from our lives for good. I don't like feeling that way, but she has taken too much from us."

"We are turning into people who want to catch and destroy. We just got married, we should be making love, making babies, and cooking dinner at home in our own kitchen. But instead we're putting ourselves out there, risking everything to put an end to this whole screwed up mess."

He takes my glass. "How about we make out heavily on the sofa?"

"You want to distract me?"

"Yes, actually I do."

"I'm in."

After our make out session on the sofa, we now lay in bed talking about the possibility of having twins or triplets. We talk about what kind of house we would like to raise our many children in, then fall asleep thinking about today. I can tell he was feeling better this morning, but as the day progressed, his concerns reappeared.

*

Standing inside the bar tonight, I felt a sense of home. I loved the 42 and I love how Michael became the boss, seeing to the details and managing the staff.

We hear a loud crash and look to see Carla has dropped a tray. She's immediately helped by two other waitresses. Everyone is working to keep the bar running smoothly tonight.

Michael is behind the bar filling orders to keep busy as I prep trays of drinks before they go out onto the floor. He smiles at me and I smile back. This is hard for him—hard for us—knowing what's at stake. He comes over with two beers and sets them on the tray.

"Have you seen anyone who might be her?"

"No, I haven't."

He reminds me of a bull—muscular and strong with flaring nostrils ready to run over anyone who comes between us. He needs to take the edge off.

I slip in to join him behind the bar and take a bottle of tequila, filling two shot glasses. I hand one to him.

"Here, drink with me."

We do and he kisses me. "PDA, remember?"

I see Carla struggling again when I step out from behind the bar to help her and I hold up one finger.

"It will take just a minute."

He doesn't like it, but he rests his hands on the bar to watch me.

"Carla, let me help you."

"Mrs. Tucker, I'm sorry. I just feel off tonight."

"It's okay. I'll give you some advice I once got. Hydrate. Then breathe. You are doing a great job, don't let anyone rush you. You know what to do."

"Thank you."

"You're welcome. Now go dump the pan, get some water, and go to the bathroom. Don't forget to pee when you can. Got it?"

"Yes, ma'am."

"Please, it's Jamie."

She leaves to do as I asked. As I walk back to the bar where Michael is still watching me, I walk into Caleb.

"You made it." I smile and kiss his cheek.

"I think the female officer outside my house might have a thing for me, so I needed to get out for a while."

"Well you *are* a catch, even without Eli in tow."

He puts his arm around me as we continue to the bar. "How's he doing?"

"Do you see that intense look on his face? He's concerned about me."

"As he should be."

We continue to the bar where my husband is wiping glasses.

"Caleb, glad you could make it," Michael says in greeting.

"It's busy in here. Outside is nuts."

Meredith walks by, eyeing Caleb. He does look different than before. He seems to stand taller, has definition to his arms, and has let his hair grow just enough. She stops in front of us not taking her eyes from him.

I speak. "Hey Meredith, are you okay?"

She takes in a deep breath. "Sure. Um, could you come to the kitchen with me, Jamie?"

I look at Michael. He doesn't like it, but nods okay only to intercede with a response he can live with.

"Caleb, let's go to the back. Want a drink? My treat."

We all make our way through the crowd looking at faces as we do, but still nothing. The two guys find a table near the kitchen as Michael hands a beer to Caleb and drinks a water. He watches me walk into the kitchen with Meredith.

She goes on and on about how good Caleb looks and would he be interested in her. I say, probably and she peeks back out at him. He sees her and just smiles a little awkward smile as Michael laughs. It's the first laugh I've heard from him since we got here today. She needs to get a tray of food out, and I rejoin the boys.

We talk over plans for Caleb and Eli to visit us in New York when we're all alerted to a noise towards the front of the bar. It seems an argument has broken out and there's a fight. The crowd moves, huddling around what's going on. Michael looks at me.

"Go. I will be here with Caleb."

He looks at Caleb. "Don't let her out of your sight."

"I won't."

He is up front in minutes, out of our range of sight. I don't want to assume the worst and I try to talk Caleb into us going up there to see what was wrong, but he keeps me safely in the back like he said he would.

Then there's a loud pop coming from the kitchen with a flash of light. Caleb grabs my hand as we go check it out. Seth, one of two cooks tonight is laying on the floor, moving around with dark singed marks on his shirt and cap. Flames are rising over the griddle. Caleb bends down to move him out the way and I grab the extinguisher. I push the lever and nothing happens. I try again.

"Are you kidding me?"

I go out to the hall where I know the other extinguisher is hanging, but it's gone. Two girls are using it to open the bathroom door. The flames are getting bigger, causing the sprinkler system to turn on. I look for Caleb who is trying to get two customers to help Seth out. He runs to the bar, grabbing another extinguisher and heads to the kitchen. He notices I'm gone then sees me heading towards the bathrooms.

"Jamie, don't!"

Smoke is beginning to fan out into the bar area when the alarm alerts everyone to evacuate. I tell the girls they need to get out of the bar, but they're all trying to speak. I grab one of them.

"Who is in there?"

"It's our friend Mandy. She broke up with her boyfriend because she saw him kissing a girl on the dance floor. She had a lot to drink. Maybe she passed out?"

Caleb comes running down the hall towards us. "The fire is out, contained in the kitchen. What's wrong?"

"Their friend locked herself inside, maybe even passed out."

The alarm is loud, and people are trying to get out of all the exits. He moves in front of the bathroom door, kicking it with his foot. He kicks it again and the second time it opens. Sure enough, the girl is laying by the sink, passed out. Caleb picks her up and the girls follow him to the door. I take a moment to be sure no one is in the men's room then run upstairs to check the office. When I'm sure all is clear back here, I head out the door.

I find Caleb coming for me. "Jamie!"

"I'm here, let's go find Michael."

We make our way with others to the front of the building. There are two fire engines, along with police cars. Caleb tugs on my arm.

"Look, there he is."

Michael stands with a police officer when he spots us. He runs his fingers through his hair and I can see the worry on his face.

He pulls me in his arms, taking a moment to look me over. "I didn't know what happened to you. They wouldn't let me back inside."

"We're okay. There was a fire in the kitchen. Caleb had to pull Seth out of the way, then he broke down the bathroom door with his foot to save a girl."

Michael looks at Caleb.

"Yeah I did that. See, I have muscles too."

Michael thanks him for getting me out safely. We all stand outside watching as the crowd slowly disperses. The fire chief says the fire was out and the damage seemed to be contained in the kitchen. There's still no reason yet as to what caused the fire. After about an hour, we're allowed back inside to look over the damage.

The sight hits Michael in the gut again and I can see the look of defeat on his face. "This might be the end of 42."

"Michael, don't say that."

Caleb speaks. "What if all this was another planned event to get you two apart?"

"It's the first thing I thought about. We're going to the Hotel, do you want to come by?"

"Naw, you both need to get some rest. Where was the security detail you guys are supposed to have when all of this was happening?"

Michael and I look at each other. He's right, where were they?

Chapter 26

Jamie

Michael and I arrive at the hotel and all I want is some hot tea to calm my frazzled disappointed self, a shower, and a bed. He's unloading his pockets on the bar when I break the silence.

"Do you want me to order you something?"

"No, water is fine."

"I'm going to make myself hot tea, so why don't you go shower?"

He starts to go to the bedroom but stops, turning around. "Jamie, I'm sorry."

"Sorry for what?"

"For holding on so tight to you. Tonight proved I can't protect you."

"No, what happened tonight has nothing to do with you protecting me. We had a series of unexpected things break out all at once. Yes, it could be Stacey's doing or it could just be life's oddities. We are trying to do so much, trying desperately to get our lives back, but the plan isn't working. It makes us more agitated waiting for something to happen. We can't go home with Pete still in the hospital and we have no freedom here because of her. None of this is normal."

I wrap my arms around him and place my ear to his chest, closing my eyes. His arms tighten around me and I feel his chin on my head. He walks us into the bedroom and I look up at him.

"What are you doing?"

He lays a finger on the tip of my nose. "I need to be with you."

I comply with his need, forgetting the hot tea, the shower, and the unpredictable world around us. Our love keeps us going, and our love will get us through what's to come.

I take my phone from my back pocket to find a song I know he likes, then remove his shirt, pushing him onto the bed. He smiles, scooting up onto the pillow. Now my canvas is before me, giving me space to work my magic fingers. I bend down to kiss him, asking him to roll over. Crawling over him, I sit across just below his hips and begin to massage my fingers into his skin, working my way up towards his waist and moving back to front. His cheek rests on his folded hands, giving me a wonderful view of his muscles. I move up to his shoulders, then down the length of his arm as his muscles respond to my touch. I apply gentle, steady pressure leaving a few precise kisses. I work my way across his back and hips, hearing the stress begin to release through his lips. It makes it hard not to cover them with mine. The song ends and leads into another, and my hands dip around to the front of his hip, causing him to stir underneath me.

He twists to face me and rests his hands on my thighs, looking at me with desire heavy eyes. His hand slips behind my head as he pulls me down to him. He gives me the kiss I want, controlled and gentle.

No words are needed as we go to the place that is all our own.

Michael

I wake up from a dream I've had many times before. Jamie is gone. But when I look to my left, she is asleep on her stomach, hugging her pillow.

Moving the sheet off me, I roll out of the bed hoping not to disturb her. I pull on sweats that lay across the chair near the bed. First to the bathroom, then on to get water from the mini fridge. I check my phone for any new messages, but there are none. I'm not sure if that's good or bad. Pulling out a water bottle, I let the cold water run down my throat. It's 3:00 in the morning as I look out over the town which is quiet except for a paper delivery van.

Out of the corner of my eye, I see Jamie standing in the doorway of the bedroom.

"Did you get cold? I see you grabbed a shirt." I ask.

She yawns, stretching her arms up over her head. Her belly peeks out from under the shirt. "I did, my warm man blanket left me."

"I'm sorry."

"What time is it?"

"After 3:00. Would you like some water?"

"Maybe a sip of yours. Are you alright?"

"I woke up from a dream."

She tilts her head, waiting for me to finish. "Was I gone?"

I nod, confirming she's right. She lays her head against my bare arm. "I'm right here." She slides my hand down over her butt. "I'm real."

"You're a funny girl early in the morning."

"What, I don't feel real?"

"No, you are, which is why we should go back to bed."

"Um, back to bed."

She turns for the bedroom with my hand in hers but I pull her back to me, not wanting to wait to kiss her. A noise at our door makes us jerk around as it suddenly opens and the two posted undercover police officers from outside enter. I step in front of Jamie.

"What the hell is going on?"

Officer Craft and Bilson replace the other officers for the overnight shift. Craft runs past us with his weapon drawn into the bedroom. Officer Bilson remains with us, looking around like someone is inside the room other than us.

I turn to face Bilson who is standing near me. "What's going on? No one else is in here."

I reach for my phone on the bar, but he pushes me. I feel Jamie's hand leave my arm when I lunge at him, but he holds the gun to my face.

"Don't move."

That's when I hear her softly say my name. I turn to her. She's blinking her eyes like she is falling asleep and she looks at a needle dangling in her arm with Craft standing behind her, smiling. She falls as he catches her. I reach for her when I feel a sting in my arm and the gun in my back. I turn to Bilson who is holding a needle in his hand.

"What do you think Craft? He's pretty big, should we stick him twice?"

I turn back to Jamie as my vision blurs. I drop to one knee seeing she is lying lifeless on the floor. I can't believe this is happening. I get up to help her, but Bilson hits me again with another needle.

Craft kneels next to Jamie, running his hand down her leg. "You're a lucky guy, look at her."

"Don't touch her!"

I attempt to reach her again, but I can't. Lying on the floor, I blink a few times trying to see Jamie, as he picks her up and walks over me. There is nothing, I can do to stop him.

Jamie

Touching my head, I sit up looking around. It's cold, dark, and I must be on a wooden floor, but where am I?

I try and think back to what happened. I was with Michael in our hotel room. I look down and feel what I'm wearing—a t-shirt and underwear, exactly what I remember. My arm is sore, and I remember being stuck with a needle. I whisper Michael's name, doing it again in hopes he is with me. I begin to crawl, calling him and reaching out to hopefully touch him. I bump into what I guess is a wall, so I use it to stand up, steadying myself. I can't see anything except a tiny trace of light coming through some cracks in the ceiling.

I begin to fumble around the space, but it seems I'm alone. A door suddenly opens, slamming against the side of a wall. Bright light causes me to shield my eyes, but I try hard to see who I am about to meet.

It's Bilson. I back away trying to hide in the darkness, but his hands grab my arms and pull me forward as I try to fight against him. He jerks me close to him.

"Stop fighting me or it won't end well for you."

He takes me into a room with a table and two chairs and to my right, I see Michael. I scream his name, pulling away from Bilson, but he jerks my arms up behind me, rendering me still. The pain stabs hard in my arms and chest.

"Okay, okay!"

He loosens his grip on me and I turn back to Michael. I'm shoved in a chair across from him as Bilson begins to tie my hands behind me. Michael's head is bent forward and I can't see his face. He's breathing, but there's blood on the floor.

"Let me give you two a few minutes alone." Bilson leaves, shutting the door behind him.

"Michael. Michael." I try scooting my chair over to him. "Sweetie, wake up, please, you have to wake up. Please, please talk to me."

He tries to open his eyes and his arms try to move as he becomes conscious of his restraints. He is wearing sweatpants with no shirt and there are visible cuts on his body. As he picks his head up, I can see his right eye is swollen.

"Michael, can you hear me?"

This time he drops his head out of sheer relief that I am fine. "Jamie, are you okay?"

"Michael, you're hurt."

"I can take more from them, I just don't want them hurting you."

"Your eye is swollen."

"That was Craft. I came out better in that fight than he did."

I hear clapping coming from behind me. My body stiffens as Stacey appears in front of me with her two hired men. This time she's a redhead dressed in all black.

"WOW, look at you. I guess our bodies do bounce back after having children. I wonder if that's a trait on our father's side? I told you little sister to leave, but I guess me shooting Josh wasn't enough to scare you." She grabs my chin with her hand.

Michael struggles behind her in the chair. "Leave her alone."

She takes a moment, then releases my chin with a jerk. Walking over to him, she blocks me from seeing him.

"Look at that, he is loyal to you. You leave him, hurt him, but he still loves you. What a bitch you are to do that to him." She smiles and walks behind him. "What did I tell you that night? If you didn't leave, I would hurt the ones you love." She puts her hand on his shoulder, running it down his chest. She puts her face next to his ear as he leans away from her.

"Fatherhood looks good on you. How old is your little boy, six or seven months?"

My eyes shoot to her. "Leave him out of this, you are pissed at me."

"You don't get it, do you? In this scenario you listen and obey. You get nothing, and I will get everything. All you had to do was stay away. Michael loved me once."

"I never loved you."

"Well, maybe you could have loved me if this cheap thrill didn't come along. Maybe I'll have you one more time before I do away with you. It's a pity to waste such a wonderful man. Craft, let's do some damage to this handsome face so my sister knows I'm serious."

"NO!"

"Oh, there you go, fighting for your man. I have others to fight for me. Craft, come here." Craft's nose is swollen, probably broken. "Why don't you give tough man here a hit for breaking your nose."

Craft pulls back his fist, hitting Michael in the jaw and throwing his head to the side.

"Stop it!"

She glares at me. "Again, but harder this time."

Craft hits him again, but this time Michael's eyes start to flutter. He squints looking at me as blood dribbles from his mouth. He spits it out.

She looks at Craft. "Doesn't that feel good?" Then to Michael, "That's for forcing the paternity test. All you had to do was accept me. Take him to the box."

They cut his ties and it takes both to pull him away. The pain in my body is nothing like the pain of seeing him take those hits. I'm screaming at them to let him go, pleading with her.

She walks over, pulling the other chair close to me.

"Lola," she says.

My eyes fall to my lap. Our suspicions were right.

"Lola saw you in New York. She said you didn't have much to say, you just ran away. She called me immediately, you know. See, it's very easy for me to have people watching anyone I want. Do you remember a little encounter with Mr. Stewart at Shaw Gallery?" She pulls out her phone. "Like this is the cutest little boy. But he has Michael's genes, so of course he is cute." She turns the phone to me.

I look at it to see my son in his father's arms on the beach. It was Michael's birthday.

"He's a child who's done nothing to you."

"Innocent right now, but when I get done raising him, he won't be."

"That will never happen."

"Let me fill you in on the details, honey. You and Michael will stay here, locked up in your private box until I decide I don't need you anymore. Everyone will now learn the truth about you."

"What?"

"That you had an affair with Caleb, and it devastated Michael. It broke him and in a jealous rage he killed you, then took his own life. His parents will die in a freak accident or from grief at losing their only son not his cheating wife. As for your son, well with all his known relatives gone, he will go to foster care. He'll be there for a little while, then I will swoop in to save him. His only living relative, Aunt Stacey. I will finally get Michael's child all to myself." She leans down close to me. "You see, neither one of you will live to see him grow up. He will inherit the Tucker wealth and I will be sitting pretty, overseeing all of it."

My eyes are fixated on her. "You're a crazy bitch who only wants what you can't have. This is my family and you won't hurt them."

I raise my legs and kick her chair, making us both fall over. She scrambles back up on her feet as she yells out.

"Bilson, Craft!"

The two come back, looking a little frazzled. They had tied my arms behind me, but not my ankles, giving me this opportunity. She holds her stomach and points with her other finger.

"Take the bitch and knock her out! I don't want her speaking to Michael or moving for hours. GO!"

Chapter 27

Michael

$\mathcal{L}$ ooking at my unconscious wife, I think:

I will do anything to get you out of here and back to Ben. You don't deserve any of this. I need you to survive whatever hell she has put you through. I know you are hurt, but I need you to open your eyes, I need to see them. I opened my eyes one day to beauty in a way I never noticed in a woman before you. Please come back to me.

There is so much I want to show you, to give to you. The other night I was thinking of what kind of vehicle we should get to haul all our little Tuckers to school in? I want to be the dad in the carpool line dropping them off before work after you've made them breakfast. Four children, that will be the number. We'll take either boys or girls because we will be blessed to have them. I want at least one girl that looks like you, whose eyes are green. Someday her boyfriends will fear me, just a little. I'll make sure they all take up for each other, that they are kind and hard working individuals. You'll be the one helping with homework and I will fix spaghetti on Friday nights. But Saturday night will be all ours, then waffles on Sunday morning with the kids.

I know we discussed waiting on getting a dog until we get into a house, but I saw a rescue the other day when I had Ben at the park. A lab named Archie. You would have fallen in love with him.

"Jamie, I need you to wake up. Please baby, wake up and come over to me. I keep pulling on these ties, but I can't get loose. Please…"

Jamie

I push up with my hands trying to steady myself. "What are they using to knock us out?"

"Jamie."

"Michael, I'm coming, where are you?"

"Follow my voice, I'm tied to a bar in the wall."

I finally lay my hands on him.

"You've been out for a while. What happened to you?"

"She said some really bad things. I got angry, then I kicked her chair, knocking her over. That's when she told them to knock me out."

"That's my girl."

"Let me see if I can untie you."

I move around him and feel tape on his wrist, not a zip tie. I crawl around, working on the tape that binds his wrist together around a pipe and after several attempts I free him. He wraps me in his arms, bringing us back together. I tighten my grip around him.

"I saw her phone."

"I did too, before they brought you into the room. Nothing she is saying will happen."

"I'm trying not to let her get to me, but I'm scared. Michael, how will we get out of here?"

He lifts my chin. "I don't know, but we will." He kisses me and I wince with pain. "I'm sorry."

The door opens, and a bag is thrown onto the floor before the door shuts. We're in the dark again. We both move towards it, but he stops me.

"Jamie, wait, let me see what it is."

He opens it to reveal a blanket and a tiny flashlight, along with a can of beans, two granola bars, and an apple. We both look at each other and take it to the wall, propping ourselves against it.

"Oh wait, there's water too. I guess she's doing what she promised, keeping us alive until she doesn't need us."

With the light on, we inspect everything to be sure it hasn't been tampered with. Then he turns the flashlight to me, his fingers touching my cheek when I ask about my face.

"How bad?"

He forces a smile.

I take the flashlight looking at his face. He's swollen under his right eye with a cut that needs attention, along with other bruises and dried blood. His shoulder might need stiches. I smile up at him.

"We've both been beaten."

"Yes, but we're still here."

I put some water on my shirt trying to clean the cut on his shoulder, then wipe off the dried blood from his face. He does the same for me.

We eat the apple, sip on some water, then huddle together waiting for the next storm surge. He holds my hand as I rest my head against his arm. We need to get some sleep, but not knowing what's next keeps us alert.

The door swings open once again and we squint, adjusting to the light. Bilson comes in pointing a gun at me. He tells Michael to stay down—I'm coming with him, then orders me to stand. The grip I have on Michael's arm loosens. He looks at me with fear in his eyes as I stand up slowly. He grabs my hand.

"I'm not letting you go with him," he says.

"And I don't want you shot. Remember, she wants to keep us for a while."

"Jamie?"

"I can do this. Promise me you won't charge at him."

His eyes divert from me to Bilson, then back to me. He doesn't want me to go, but he doesn't want me hurt if he attacks Bilson.

"Do what you have to do."

I walk out the door with Bilson, looking back at Michael.

They have me sit in a chair opposite of her with a metal table between us. They didn't tie me this time which leaves me to wonder what's planned for me. She leans her elbows on the table just staring at me.

"I have a proposition for you."

I say nothing.

"I've been watching you both on the camera in your storage locker and I figured out that getting Ben to be my son will take longer if I don't have one of you, so I need a new plan. Bilson, kill Jamie."

I jump out of my chair, turning to see Bilson standing with his arms crossed and resting on his chest. My heart is beating so fast, I stumble into the table as she pushes it into me.

"Take a seat Jamie, just playing. Bilson, give my sister a bottled water. I don't need her passing out on me yet."

I don't realize I'm still standing until he pushes me down in the seat, handing me a bottle.

"Don't worry, it's safe to drink. Okay, back to my proposition. Pete, as you know, is in the hospital. Before he had his unfortunate illness, he signed over his share in the 42 to me."

"No, he wouldn't do that."

"Yes, he did. I started planning my attack on Pete before Michael left town the last time. Little did I know he would find you and not return for a while, which was a blessing for me, giving me full access to the bar. Pete was easy to fool."

"What did you do to him?"

"When you get close to someone, it's easy to drop medicine in their food or drink. Pete was under stress. I think he was having a little mid-life crisis. It was easy to show him my nice side."

"You poisoned him?"

"Yes."

"I saw pictures of you as Kimber."

"Now that was brilliant on my part. I dressed down but stayed hot and changed my hair color. I added some glasses and apparently, I was no longer

Stacey. I became Kimber. But let me get back to my story. I followed him up to the office one night to retrieve a bottle of scotch for a bachelor party, when I saw your picture on the desk. I asked him who you were and all he said was that you were a family friend. I just didn't know where you were. The day Lola called me changed my plan, but that was okay, because our worlds were about to crash and burn."

She throws papers at me. "Look them over. It's all legal."

"He wouldn't do this."

"What is wrong with you? How do you get through life thinking everyone is perfect? Let me lay down some real for you. Remember that freak accident I told you about way back when you were to disappear, never to see Michael again? That reality, sweetheart, is a phone call away and unfortunately your little Ben might be with his grandparents when it happens."

"You're lying."

"No, I'm not. In fact, let me show you what I mean." She picks up her phone.

"Why would you want to harm an innocent child? He belongs to Michael. You said you loved him once, how could you do this to him?"

She looks down at her phone then up at me. "I wanted him to love me, but he didn't. Not like he loves you. I thought our life together would be perfect because we were both broken, but you came along and my chance to win him back was destroyed."

She turns her phone so I can see my apartment building. People are walking, cars are going down the street.

"Stacey, please don't do this."

I see a momentary hesitation in her eyes, until she takes away the phone and sends a text. "Done."

"What, what did you do?" This time I scream at her. "Tell me what you did!"

"I put my guy on standby. If you and Michael do not cooperate with everything I ask for, I will do the unthinkable."

I see nothing but my hands around her neck. I jump out of my chair, knocking it behind me, and lunge across the table, falling with her onto the floor.

I start hitting her, wanting to kill her. She's threatened my family and for what, money?

"Get off of me, GET HER OFF OF ME!"

We're tangled up in the table, the fallen chair, and each other when she yells at Bilson. I feel two hands on my shoulders, but I have a tight grip around her neck. I felt nothing but rage, and I want it to end. I wanted her dead. Her fist punches into my side as I lose my grip on her. His hands come around my waist as he pulls me off her, but I continue to kick and punch. She stands up.

"You bitch! Where the hell were you Bilson? I pay you good money to protect me. Take her back. Get Craft, we're moving up the plan, tonight."

She comes over to where he is holding me. "Enjoy a few more hours with your husband, because soon neither of you will exist to be a problem for me. Now get her out of my sight," she orders Bilson.

I'm shoved through the door, caught by Michael. I throw my arms around him as crying overtakes me. He tries to assess but holds me close, trying to calm me. He places his hand behind my head.

"Jamie, breathe in, out. Come on, listen to my voice. Breathe in, then out."

I begin to do it, bringing me back to the horrible place I've just gone.

"That's it, can you tell me what happened?"

"I jumped across the table at her. My hands were on her neck. I could have killed her, I hate what she is doing."

"Come over and sit with me."

I tell him every detail of the meeting with her. I tell him about what's going on with Pete and the contract that signed over Pete's shares to her. I tell him about the waiting car outside of the apartment in New York.

"If something happens to them, it will be my fault. I shouldn't have reacted so violently."

He cradles me in his arms, running his hand over my hair trying to soothe me but I'm sure I've sealed their fate. All I can see is my son's innocent face. I can't stop crying, my body shaking. Michael wraps the blanket around me.

"I need you to listen to me."

I look up at him, wanting his words to relieve my concerns and take away the pain my heart feels. He leans in as close as he can to whisper in my ear, telling me to wrap my arms around him, as though he's comforting me. He tells me to kiss him, which I do. He kisses my neck as my hair covers his face. Then he tells me what measures he and his father put into place. When I need to look into his eyes for reassurance, I do as he wipes away tears off my cheek. When he's done, I begin to cry. He's taken care of us, our son, and his parents. He can't change what we're going through, but he made sure they're all safe. I look into his beautiful brown eyes and lay my head against his. I whisper, "Thank you."

I sit on his lap and wrap the blanket around us both, feeling the air come back into my lungs. I can breathe again.

We fall asleep sitting upright against the wall when the door flies open once again. He stands and pushes me behind him, but this time they take him, leaving me to bang on the door until my fists are swollen, and blood runs down my arm. I move away from the door and look up at this horrible place, then scream as loud as I can, for as long as I could.

I'm not sure how long it has been since they took him, but the fear of what's happening to him makes me sick. I begin to heave, holding myself up against the walls as my head spins. Moving is my only hope to stay awake and I pace, then purge myself in the corner. Where is he? What is she doing to him?

I hear the familiar sound of the door opening and I stand, hoping it's Michael. It's not. Craft comes inside alone.

"Where is my husband?" I walk towards him as he smiles, tossing a bag onto the floor.

"Eat, I have plans for us."

"Where is Michael?"

He disappears as fast as he came.

I open the bag. There is a bottle of water, a pudding cup, and a picture. I fall onto the floor as I silently cry without sound. I'm holding my breath unable to breathe. I slam the bag against the wall and let out a sound I can't distinguish. I fall into a fetal position, not knowing if what I see is real. When I'm able to look at it again, I do.

Michael

I fight against them as they both try to fasten me to the chair, but the gun resting in my back makes me stop. It's not about me getting shot, but if I get shot, I can't help Jamie. She is always going to be the woman who gives me strength, so staying strong for her is what I need to do. That's when I feel the pierce of a needle in my arm. Everything begins to darken.

When I wake up, I realize I'm in a chair. Stacey appears next to me, her hand on my shoulder.

"Ready to talk?"

"What do you want?"

"I want your wife to suffer."

"You're a sick bitch!"

"Yeah well, I don't care what you think anymore. When I loved you…"

"That's bull. You don't know how to love anyone but yourself."

She begins to clap. "Nice. But I did love you. When I came back from Italy, I thought you would see me, forget all the things I did, and want me back. But as it turns out, you had moved on to my little sister. That still sounds weird. I know she told you that Pete signed over his shares to 42, which you are going to tell me is not real, but it is. I have papers here for you to sign over your shares as well as all claims to your family business and naming me Ben's guardian."

"I'm not signing anything."

"You will because I have someone ready to make an accident happen to your parents as well as your precious son. If that's not enough to make you want to sign everything you own over to me, then maybe I should show you what your wife is doing right now."

She turns her phone around and I see Jamie laying on the floor. She is curled up, crying and shaking.

"What did you do to her?"

"You can thank Bilson. She thinks you're dead."

"What?"

"She saw a picture of you slumped over on the floor. I didn't say you were dead, but you look dead."

"Why do you want to hurt her? She didn't do anything to you."

She looks at me, contemplating her answer and that's when I see a tear fall onto her cheek as she wipes it away.

"That's sort of true. I grew up with parents who weren't present. One was in love with someone else and too drunk most of the time to be able to look at me. The other one had the means to find what he wanted, but I'm not sure he ever cared about her. One time I saw him try and kiss her, but she looked like it hurt.

I had nannies, instructors, and drivers to take me anywhere and give me whatever I wanted. They did what my daddy paid them to do. No discipline, no love, just robotic actions towards a child who turned into a teenager without boundaries, giving me the world at my fingertips. Finding out my mother had an affair made things clearer about how they acted towards each other."

"If you had a picture, why didn't you go in search of him?"

"I didn't need him. I needed to get my father out of the picture and take control of our family wealth. That's when I began to dabble in drugs of persuasion to manipulate people to do what I want. With him secured in Italy, it was time for me to find you. You took to me right away. I guess I fed your bad side, your rebellious nature. I wanted what your family had. Combining our families together would bring me the power I craved. Just to let you know, I never used drugs on you. I found you to be challenging in every way possible."

She touches my cheek and I turn away from her.

"I cheated on you when you started wanting better things for yourself. You were broken and needy, but I loved you anyway. You started turning away from me, but I had needs too.

When I came back to Hopson from being with my dad, I saw you. The look in your eyes was different. I thought winning you back would be easy, but you loved her, which made me hate her for taking you from me. When I found out about our connection as sisters, I only wanted to break her like she broke my family. I couldn't get revenge on her father because he was dead, but I could make her pay for what he did.

Jamie had the life I always craved. She got you and now Ben. She disappeared for a year and you took her back, loving her more than ever. I see the two of you on the camera in your locker and I want that connection with you.

So now you see, I have no choice. It's simple. I know you will never want to be with me and raise Ben as ours. There is no way in hell I will let her have a happily-ever-after, so I need to make a decision."

"Which is?"

"Who will watch the other die."

I spend many hours sitting in that chair, not knowing what is going on with Jamie. She's crumpled on the floor grieving for me, but I'm alive, so close to her. I yell her name, over and over, but no one comes to quiet me, nor can I hear her. Closing my eyes, I think of her. She is beside me laying in the bed in our cottage. The wind is blowing her hair, and her suntanned leg escapes the covers, leaving my fingers to run over her skin before she wakes up. I'm in love with her and this will not be the end of us. I believe in our forever, whatever it takes.

*

Jamie

It's been a while since I saw or heard anyone, but my body was stiff from laying on the floor. He can't be dead, this must be another one of her cruel jokes.

There's a loud noise on the other side of the door. I know this is it. She's coming for me next. I push myself up, knowing my fight is about to begin. I'm not going the way she intends me to go.

There's another loud noise like someone had been thrown against the door. I make a fist, plant my feet, and am ready to fight. The door flies open and Craft points his gun into the room. I huddle next to the wall close to the opening. There's a shot and I see him jerk. He spins as another shot rings out and he drops to the floor with a horrible thud. My body is shaking violently—I don't know what's happening.

Then I see Michael standing in the light from the other side of the door.

"Michael?"

Caleb steps into the room holding a gun as Michael pushes ahead of him, coming to me.

"Jamie!"

I jump into his arms and he holds me close to him, then pulls away to look at me to be sure I'm alright and I do the same for him. I wrap my arms around his neck, not wanting to ever let him go. I open my eyes to see Caleb, who lets out the breath he's holding.

"Caleb, what are you doing here and why do you have a gun?"

I see a police officer behind him, who speaks into his shoulder radio. He tells them one assailant is dead, two have been captured, and the two hostages have been located, alive.

"I'll explain everything soon, but right now you both need to get out of here and be seen by EMT's."

Michael assists me as we step around the body on the floor. There are a lot of lights and police officers in both uniform and plainclothes.

I touch Caleb's arm. "Do we know if Ben and the Tucker's are safe?"

"Yes, they are safe. The person outside the apartment has been apprehended as well."

We're outside in the ambulance being examined when Chief Johnson comes over.

"Mrs. Tucker, Mr. Tucker. I'm sorry if Caleb couldn't tell you anything. We've had a case going with Bilson and Craft for inappropriate dealings inside the department for a while now. While investigating, Kimber was seen meeting them on several occasions. When Pete got sent to the hospital and they said he was poisoned, we started watching her more closely. We found her almost everywhere you two were while in town. I'm sorry we didn't find you sooner."

Michael addresses Caleb. "So, you're a police officer?"

"Yes, it's the only way to protect my son and be prepared for anything. I joined the academy when my second year of college was done. I'm sorry I couldn't say anything."

I smile over at him as Chief Johnson continues. "There was a cleaning lady at the hotel who was taking a smoke break about the time you both were taken out. She reported it to her boss. He didn't believe her at first, until he saw the black van on the camera at the back of the hotel. He called us right away. We have questions for the both of you but first you'll be going to the hospital and then questioned briefly. You both need time, but I would like to see you at the station tomorrow."

Michael stands, shaking his hand. "Thank you."

As Chief Johnson walks away, I make my way over to Caleb and wrap my arms around his neck. "Thank you."

I can feel his shoulders relax. "I'm glad you are alright."

Michael joins us, wrapping his arms around us both. "The family is back together."

At the hospital, we're checked out by a doctor. Michael received stitches in his shoulder along with antibiotics. We're asked some questions, given clean clothes after samples are given, along with bottles of water.

As promised, Caleb drives us back to our hotel, then walks us up to our new room. We get a few odd looks from people in the hotel and a huge apology from the manager.

"Your clothes are in suitcases. You can call room service and order whatever you want. I'll be by tomorrow before taking you to the station, so maybe we can catch lunch after the interview."

Michael takes his hand to shake it, then he grabs him in a hug. I step up too.

"You're a mystery to me right now, but I'm not sure how we could ever truly thank you for everything you have done."

"We've all been through a lot, but she's not getting away this time. I want you both in Eli's life, in my life. I want Ben to know me as Uncle Caleb. It has a good ring to it, doesn't it?"

"You have a special place in my heart always." I rise to kiss his cheek.

"I love you too, always have." He looks at Michael. "I love you too, big guy."

*

Caleb leaves us in our room and we immediately head for the shower, stripping out of the scrubs they gave us at the hospital. We finally have time to be alone and assess the physical damage from the past few days.

The hot water feels like liquid magic mixed with the pleasant familiar smell of body wash. Michael stops at a bruise on my side with the sudsy sponge, placing a kiss on my shoulder. His finger touches my face, then he places a kiss on my forehead. He's hurting for me, seeing the results of the ordeal we just went through. There are other bruises and cuts, but everything will heal. He also has bruises, cuts that required stitches, but his pain is for me.

"There is nothing you wouldn't do for me or for our son, is there?" He chokes up before getting out the last word.

I pull his face down to me, kissing him and holding on as tight as I can. When he wraps his arms around me, I wince with pain and he lets go.

"I'm sorry, it's just, I was trying to…"

I touch his face. "I'm fine. I was so scared she had…"

He kisses my cheek. "I didn't know what they had done to you, and when I saw you curled up on the floor, that was worse than any pain they inflicted on me."

"But we made it."

His fingers brush the side of my wet hair. "May I?"

"Of course."

He backs me up to feel the full force of the shower running through my hair, and he begins to wash it. When he's done, I do the same for him.

After the shower, we brush our teeth and slide into clean clothes and bed. We know our family is safe, we're safe, and she's in jail. There is nothing else to keep us from having the life we've wanted, the life we choose.

Chapter 28

Michael

wake up first this morning in some pain but not enough to stir me out of bed and away from Jamie. I slept hard and I think she did too. She's breathing steadily with the occasional moan escaping her lips when she changes positions. I move her hair from over her eyes, letting it fall over her back when I see her peek at me. She turns over stretching and the expression on her face lets me know her body is feeling everything from the past few days.

She raises her head to kiss me. "How long have you been awake?"

"Not long. How are you feeling?"

She goes to set up. "Sore mostly. You?"

"Better since seeing that smile on your face. Do you want some juice?"

"We have juice?"

"Yes, along with a variety of muffins, danishes, and croissants."

"You ordered?"

"Nope, there was a knock, then a woman with a cart of food, compliments of Caleb."

"Aw, that's sweet and sounds delicious. What can I bring you?"

"How about we go, get it, and bring it back to bed?"

"I like your plan. Let me go to the bathroom, then I'll be right out."

After eating breakfast, we get dressed and I'm in front of the mirror, fastening my jeans. He joins me, placing his hands on my hips.

"Nice shiner," I say to him.

He takes a closer look at my face. "How do you make a swollen bruised cheek look hot?"

I start to laugh, but wince at the pain in my cheek and my side. He pulls up my shirt and kisses my skin, causing an outbreak of goosebumps as a small giggle escapes my mouth. He places another one, moving up and kissing my chest at the opening of my blouse. I lean my head back, taking in the feeling as he makes his way to my neck. He tips my chin down, placing his mouth on mine ever so softly so as not to worsen the bruises and cuts we both have. My arms wrap around his neck, wanting to feel more when his phone vibrates in his pocket.

"You better get it."

He reaches into his pocket, holding my gaze. "Yes Caleb, what do you want? We're up and I'll be right there."

"He's at the door?"

Michael puts his phone away, kissing me again. "Sooner we get done with all of this, the sooner we can get back in that bed."

After a couple of hours at the station we meet at Carol's Grille for lunch and to catch up with our secret agent friend.

Sliding into a booth, we're immediately met with a red headed waitress in her 40's. "Well I know this handsome cutie right here, but who is your friend and this beautiful woman sitting with you today?"

"Farley, this is Michael and Jamie. They're good friends of mine," Caleb says.

She looks at us both. "The two of you were on the news this morning. I'm glad you're okay."

We both thank her.

"Now, what can I get you all?"

We place our order with Farley who brings us back a pot of coffee along with biscuits.

Caleb fills us in on being a police officer. He plans on staying with his parents for another year, giving Eli a family that loves him and stability. Not to mention the free babysitting. We speak about our new plans of going back and doing things without looking over our shoulders or coming back to Hopson without fearing confrontation. We are all breathing easier today.

We leave Caleb with a bag of chocolate chip cookies Farley thought Eli needed and we make a pact that our families will stay connected, visit, and let our children know they always have family who loves them.

*

Today we arrive at the hospital with no police presence or ID checks necessary and enter the elevator with everyone else. Michael squeezes my hand and pulls me close to him.

The doors open and we spot Lacy first. Her mouth drops open, as she begins to cry before pulling me into a tight hug. She then touches Michael's arm and hugs him too.

"Oh my God, you both have been through so much. Look at you!"

I grin. "We're free."

She takes my hand. "Yes, you are. Pete is awake, sitting up in bed, waiting for you both. Thank you for coming when he needed you most. You know that you are a part of our family; Pete already thinks of you both as his kids."

Michael nods. I know the word "family" brings such different emotions than it did when he was growing up.

"Lacy, we'll be going home soon," he says, "but you guys can call us anytime."

She touches his hand. "I know. Go, go see him."

We open the door to find Pete sitting up in bed with a tray in front of him. He runs his hand over his buzzed head.

"Get over here, you two."

The closer we get, the more obvious it is that he's choking back his emotions, trying not to cry.

I hug him as tight as I can. "You gave us quite the scare."

He just looks at my face, shaking his head. "I'm sorry you got hurt."

"I'm fine."

"Michael, your face looks the same."

We all laugh through our tears, knowing how bad this could have been. He wipes his face with a tissue I hand him.

"Is it over? Do you and Jamie get your life back?" he asks us.

"Yes. She is in jail. No one will have to endure her threats anymore."

"Good. I was a stupid old man. I should have recognized who she was. Hell, I've been around her enough, you'd think…"

Michael sits in the chair next to him. "She was drugging you. You weren't yourself. The staff, your family, they all told us how different you've been. She confessed it to Jamie. When you're feeling better, we'll sit and talk about everything."

Pete shakes his head. "When are you leaving? I know this little lady needs to see her son."

"I do. We miss him."

He waves me over. "Take care of yourself, and that one. I love you."

"I love you too."

He motions to Michael. "You too, big guy."

Michael stands looking at his partner. "I want you to take it easy, maybe go on a vacation. The 42 will need repairs, so it won't be open right away. I'll get the contractors set up, and you can oversee the repairs, but you are not to do them."

Pete smiles at Michael. "I don't want to see you go, but I know you're going to be fine."

I blow Pete a kiss and we leave him to tend to the other business at hand today, the 42.

Back in New York…

It's about 12:30 in the morning when we arrive at the loft. We had a few delays before leaving Hopson. I requested a swab to prove if Stacey and I are truly sisters, but her lawyer is taking longer than expected. We'll get the results in the mail in a few weeks.

The inside of the apartment is quiet with random flashes from the TV. We breathe in and smile. His parents are standing behind the sofa waiting for us.

Laura seems visibly drained, her hands covering her mouth and Harrison has removed his glasses, rubbing his eyes. We went through hell, and it was felt by others many miles away. She comes towards her son, hugging him as tight as she could.

"Mom, I'm fine. We are fine."

"I know, but it's good to have you here where I can touch you."

Harrison hugs me, then we're all hugging.

"Laura, let her breathe," Harrison says after a bit. "I'm sure they both want to see Ben."

She wipes her eyes as her husband puts his arm around her. Michael and I go to Ben's room, just wanting a glimpse of our son. As we expected, he's safe in his bed sleeping soundly.

Coming back out to where his parents are, Michael puts his arm around me. "Jamie and I owe you both so much. I promise that we will be staying home for a while, but we want to send you both on a much-needed vacation. Keeping a seven-month-old baby and not knowing if we were going to make it back was difficult, I'm sure."

"We won't take no for an answer," I add. "We love you both so much."

Laura takes my hand, I take Michael's and he grabs his dad's, joining us in a circle. Harrison speaks up for us all.

"You both mean so much to us. We are a family who supports each other. And yes, we will take that vacation."

We all laugh at his comment, loving what we have together. When his parents leave us to go get some well-deserved sleep, we make our way down the hall to peek at Ben one more time before going to bed ourselves.

I smile looking at our perfect little boy. "He is the best of both of us."

"That he is."

Ben moves, one leg stretching outside of the blanket. I reach down and pull it over him.

"Michael—when I think of what might have happened."

"We made it."

"Yes, we did."

*

The soreness is a little better when I wake up this morning—the swelling has gone down. I roll over to see Michael looking at me.

"How is it you always wake before me?"

"It's my opportunity to look at you. I like the little drool you have going on as well."

I punch him. "Stop, that's not sexy at all."

He kisses me and it feels so good that I move closer to him, wanting to feel all that is my husband. My body is feeling better and craving his touch. He moves over me, supporting himself on his arms and letting me feel the weight of him but still cautious not to hurt me.

My hands grip his arms and slide over to his bare chest, feeling the muscles flex under my fingers. Our lips find each other, deepening the need we both have, but he stops.

I hold my breath, listening. Michael hears Ben, who seems to be moving in his bed. He kisses my neck, then looks at me.

"Want to go get him?"

I shake my head. He begins to move when I pull him down for one more long loving kiss with a promise to continue later.

*

I pull on a sweatshirt coming out of the bathroom and hear Michael talking to Ben.

"Whoa buddy, you need a diaper."

I enter the nursery to see Michael holding Ben in the air and kissing his chubby cheeks.

"Hey little guy."

Ben holds out his arms, lunging for me. I kiss him again and again. My world has become lighter just seeing his face.

I go about changing his diaper as Michael entertains him with his funny faces. We tell him we've missed him and tell him over and over how much we love him. Our little family is back together.

After diaper duty, we make coffee, fix food and leisurely enjoy our morning, taken today off to spend with our son. After breakfast we play on the floor, read books, and watch some very important shows about farm animals. Ben falls asleep sitting in his father's arms.

Michael's phone vibrates off the table and he grabs it, mouthing it's Carson's. I take Ben putting him down in his crib as Michael scurries off to his office, then I go see what's up.

He is behind the desk still on the phone, so I stand in front of the window looking out at the busy people below. When he is done, I crawl onto his lap.

"Any issues at the bar?"

"None that won't wait until tomorrow."

"Ben is asleep."

"So, we have some time alone?"

"Yes. I'm in need of your healing powers."

He lifts me up to sit on the desk in front of him. "You might have to show me what you need." He reaches over hitting a button to lower the shades behind us.

"Nice feature you insisted upon," I say.

"Should I begin my examination, Mrs. Tucker?"

"Um, please do."

Chapter 29

Jamie
Two months later…

 sit at a little café' in the city waiting for Susan to arrive. She's in town to pick out a wedding dress and to find one for me, her matron of honor. The wedding is right around the corner in Vegas, so I'm sure these dresses will represent the wild child that lives inside of her.

Sipping on a chocolate martini makes me want another, but a call from the nanny makes me wait on ordering.

"Hey Becca, what's up?"

"Ben was walking across the floor, tripped over a truck, and hit his head on a block. He has a tiny little bump but seems fine. I thought you should know."

"I'm sure with your nursing background, you did everything that needed to be done. Let me know if anything changes. Michael will be home about 4:00 this afternoon. Call if you need me."

"Thank you Jamie."

"Give him a hug from me. Thanks, Becca."

I hang up, then text Michael what happened, joking that I'm going to stop and buy Ben a helmet. He sends back a laughing emoji. I guess he's on the final plane back to the city and I can't wait to get my hands on him. His trip to the other bars this time was harder on us both, but it's what we must do for a while. I go to order another martini when I see her. Susan is wearing a black coat, black skinny jeans, and heeled boots. She looks happy.

We hug like we haven't seen each other in forever, though she came to New York a week after Michael and I returned from Hopson just to make sure we were okay. She's always been more than a sister to me, and now she has a brother-in-law and nephew. I love seeing our family grow.

"Girl, you look good," I say. "What can I order you?"

"Whatever you're drinking." She picks my glass up and takes a sip. "Delicious. You look amazing."

"Wounds are healed, and I feel great. We're really doing this today? Picking out your wedding dress?"

"Yep, I'm getting married." She begins to beat on the table with her hands causing people around us to look.

"Is he this over-the-top delirious like you?" I tease.

"He says he's lucky to find someone that's beautiful, smart, and willing to live with a doctor and his odd schedule."

"You both will make it work. It's just for a little while longer."

"Where are we going today?"

"First, I need lingerie or just a string of lace because I've not seen Michael for two weeks. Then off to Maura's, Abernathy's, and to see Savannah."

"I'm totally in." Our martini's arrive. "I can't believe you guys are going out with us tonight. Am I going to catch you having sex in the bathroom or something?"

"Can't be sure of that, but I will try and hold off until we return home. We wouldn't miss being with you guys tonight, besides Michael agreed to us going out.

"We missed you guys. You're not pregnant because you're drinking," she observes.

"No, I'm trying to be patient and not freak out about it."

"It will happen. He's not upset about it, is he?"

"No, not at all. It came so easy the first time."

"Your husband loves you, you love him. It will happen." Susan touches my hand.

I hold up my glass. "To my best girlfriend, my sister. Here's to a successful day of wedding dress shopping."

"YES!" We both cheer.

Our trip is very successful. She found and fell in love with a trumpet/mermaid sweetheart dress with beaded sequins outlining the strapless bodice. It fit her body perfectly and was beautiful on her. She cried and I cried, which told us it was the right one.

It's now 5:30 and time to head home to get dressed for tonight. I grab a cab for her.

"Michael and I will meet you at Starlings Steakhouse at 7:00, then we will go to Shine for drinking and dancing. Susan, it's a beautiful dress. You'll be a vision in white."

She hugs me. "Thank you and I will see you later. Love you."

At the apartment, I find Michael on the floor playing with Ben. Becca has gone home. My face lights up when I see him. I've missed him so much. He comes to meet me taking my dress bag and purse and takes me into his arms, kissing me back to life.

"That was a long trip."

I smile up at him. "Too long."

"What's in the little bag?"

"You'll see. Are you sure you want to go out tonight?"

"No, but yes. It's time to celebrate Susan and Thomas. It'll be fun."

My phone lights up. It's Susan. "She's telling me to wear something hot tonight."

"I like her suggestion."

"Fill me in, how was your trip?"

"Productive, lonely without you. Next time you go with me. Sleeping without you sucks."

"That's so sweet. And yes, I feel the same. I took up a relationship with your pillow."

He pulls me playfully into his arms, bending me back and kissing my neck. "Sounds scandalous. Pete sends his love."

"How is he doing?"

"He lost ten pounds and started running. The renovations look fantastic. Thanks for sending those drawings. The new oak bar is beautiful."

"I can't wait to see it in person. Why don't you go shower, then we can switch off?"

"How about Ben showers with me?"

"You're such a good daddy."

He scoops up Ben. "Just wait until later, because Daddy is in need of some momma time."

He disappears down the hall with Ben, I'm feeling a little flushed by what he said. I do love that man.

While he's gone, I tuck the little red bag away and then I'm off to fix dinner for Ben. I can hear splashing along with squeals of happy times as well as a distress call for mom. I guess water in the tub or shower relaxes Ben as well. When Michael is done with cleaning the shower and himself, we switch.

I use his favorite peony shower gel and blow dry my hair, leaving it loose. My makeup is clean and simple, but my lips are a sultry violet. I slip into a black mini dress that gathers at the neck, leaving my shoulders and part of my back exposed. Taking one last look in the mirror, I grab my purse, ready to head out when Michael comes into the bedroom with Ben.

My husband is more than sexy in gym shorts and a t-shirt but put him in black pants and a white button-down shirt and my already beating heart cranks up even more, speaking to other parts of me. He whistles and Ben looks at him.

"Jamie, you're killing me."

"You insisted we go out tonight. What do you think?" I twirl in my dress, so he can see it all. "What do you think Ben, does Dad approve?"

"In more ways than one." He smiles, his eyes dancing with excitement.

"Good, because I went a little over the top."

I can see him taking in a smell lingering in the room. I step over to him. His nose finds its way to my exposed shoulder up my neck.

I giggle, loving his attention. "Will you help me with my bracelet?"

He sets Ben on the floor to assist me. My eyes travel up the front of his shirt with the best "come get me look" I can manage.

"You smell good too."

"Is this a game we're playing tonight?"

"Whatever do you mean?"

"Who's going to lose themselves and cause a scene or pay off the driver to wait outside the car?"

"You just went there, didn't you?"

"I did." He holds out his hand. "Deal?"

I do the same. "Deal."

We seal it with a kiss. The doorbell rings signaling that PJ has arrived to take care of Ben while we're out. She's a 16-year-old who babysits Ben at night so Becca can have time off. I open the door to let her in.

"Mrs. Tucker, you look hot in that dress."

"Good—that's my intention," I reply.

She sees Michael with Ben coming into the living room. She has a goofy smile on her face.

"Hey, hello Mr. Tucker."

"Hello, PJ. Here you go—he's been bathed. It wasn't a pleasant sight."

She takes Ben. "Okay, bottle as usual?"

Michael slips on my coat. "Yes. I left you chocolate cake with almond milk. Enjoy."

"Thank you and have a good time."

I kiss Ben on the cheek. "We will."

Chapter 30

*N*o sooner than the elevator doors close, Michael moves in front of me and places his hands on my hips under my coat. He blows next to my ear, ever so softly where the hairs on my skin stand at attention. I lean back as he kisses and teases me. I like his game tremendously.

The bell pings, but he doesn't let go of his hold on me. A couple from the second-floor walks into the elevator as Michael leans against the wall. The bell pings again, stopping at the lobby. His hand slips down to grab mine and we walk off the elevator onto the sidewalk to wait for the car.

I hold his hand to my chest. "Did I tell you how much I missed you while you were gone?"

"Yes, you did and I'm looking forward to showing you later how much I've missed you."

He looks away from me and at the blue car pulling up to the curb. The driver rolls down the front passenger window.

"Mr. Tucker? I'm Andrew."

"Nice to meet you," Michael says, bending down to the driver's level. "After you, my sweet."

I crawl into the back of the car as he climbs in behind me, placing a warm hand on my bare leg as the car pulls off.

The steak house is delicious. Thomas seems like a great guy who is into Susan with all his heart. She has more than stars in her eyes for him. We talk over the Vegas plans for the wedding. It will be just the four of us, as his brother's wife is expecting and due the week before the wedding. His parents don't enjoy flying, but Susan and Thomas are going to spend time with them after enjoying a few days together in Vegas.

We arrive at Shine heading inside to grab a table, then order drinks. As we wait, I notice Susan is shaking her bottom at Thomas. He notices, of course, but doesn't move. He smiles, seeming a little awkward.

Michael leans into me. "I don't think he dances."

"Maybe he just needs to loosen up is all. I'll take her out on the floor once the shots arrive. Can you work on him?"

"Sure."

The waitress places four shot glasses of tequila in front of us and we throw them back. I make a motion to Susan to join me out on the floor. She nods, peeling off her coat and handing it to Thomas.

I wink at Michael then leave the two men alone.

Michael

"They could be at this for a while. Do you dance?" I ask.

"Be at what? And not really."

"Look at your fiancé and Jamie together. Watch Susan as she looks over at you. She's dancing for you."

"I'm not confident on the dance floor."

I catch a waitress and order more drinks for the table. "You don't have to be a good dancer. You just have to go out and make love to her without getting arrested."

He laughs then looks at them dancing. After a few minutes of seeing Susan move around so freely, he looks back at me.

"I need more shots."

"They're on the way."

"Is this why women dance together?"

"I can't speak for all women, but when you're in love with the woman dancing in front of you, it means something different to me."

"Because you love her?"

"Yes. All the women out here are dancing, but when Jamie dances, she's all mine and captivates all of me."

The waitress sets down four more shots with four beers. Thomas turns up his shot which the girls must have noticed because they come to the table.

Jamie stands next to me, breathing heavily and pulls her hair up off her neck.

"It's warm out there or it's you watching me."

She kisses me. Not a peck, but a kiss that could end this night out quickly. I hold up her shot glass.

"Thirsty?"

"Yes, please."

We take the shot and I capture her mouth before all the tequila is gone, not letting it slip away so fast. I can feel the heat escaping through her dress. I give in, kissing her sweet mouth until she needs air.

"I'm so happy you're home. Want to dance?"

"Yes."

I look over at Thomas and he turns up his beer, drinking it fast. As Jamie leads me out to the dance floor, I look at him. He shakes his head like he's about to do something and score, he does! He's taking Susan by the hand and out to the dance floor. Jamie sees them pass us, heading to the middle of the floor.

"Did you help him gain the courage?"

"I like to think his beautiful fiancé inspired him."

My attention though, is now on my wife. She moves around me with such grace, exuberance, and tiger-like confidence. I love her game.

About an hour later we all decide to head over to Carson's for a night cap and maybe some barbeque nachos. Finding a table to seat our ladies, Thomas and I go to the back to make the nachos and order some drinks.

Jamie

"Hey, what's with the face?"

Susan has a look that doesn't worry me, just makes me wonder what she's thinking about.

"He makes me so happy."

"Yes, he does. That's why you're marrying him."

Tears fill her eyes. "I just never knew I could be this happy with someone like him. He likes to read medical journals when he's not working. He likes to play video games and eat organic foods."

"He looks at you with love in his eyes. He delivers babies, is there a better job than that?"

"I love smelling like him after he has showered. I even think he's sexy in his scrubs."

"Your smile is beautiful. I'm happy you found each other."

She takes my hand. "You mean the world to me. You know, that right?"

"I do." I wave between us with my free hand. "This right here is for life. You are my sister and I love you."

We both embrace each other when the guys came out with our food and drinks. They look confused when we wipe away tears, but it doesn't take them long to realize why.

Michael and I put them in a cab, sending it to their hotel and catch one of our own. The September air at night is chilly, giving me more reasons to huddle close to my husband.

Chapter 31

Jamie

I pay the babysitter and catch up on Ben's night. She lives just down the hall, so Michael goes to the door making sure she gets home alright. Having a sitter in your building is truly a genius move on our part. I check in on Ben. He's so sweet, probably dreaming of food. That's when I drool in my sleep, anyway.

I love you little man. Sleep well my angel.

I enter the living room to get water and catch a glimpse of Michael standing by the fireplace. His hands rest in his pockets and his shirt is unbuttoned, lying slightly open. He's lit the fireplace so a light glow spreads over his body.

"You're very handsome, my love. And you're making me warm from the sight of you."

"Sure it's not the fireplace?"

I open his shirt with my finger, exposing his bare skin, and leaving behind a kiss.

"Why do you think we're not pregnant yet?"

"Jamie, please don't worry about it."

"The first time was so easy. We weren't even trying."

"I'm enjoying our family the way it is right now. We will have more children, someday. We've been through a lot. Maybe the universe is letting us slow down, and just take it all in."

"Will you be happy if we only have Ben?"

"Yes, of course I will. I just thought you wanted more right away." He pulls me in, kissing the top of my head.

"I do want more children, but maybe not being pregnant right now is good."

"We can keep perfecting our baby making technique."

"Oh, I like that. You, my husband, are a genius."

"I'm going to get us some water." He kisses my nose.

He steps around into the kitchen where he can't see me. I undo my dress, allowing it to puddle at my feet.

"Jamie, I don't want to take these trips anymore. I know I'm complaining but I've missed you."

He comes back into the living room and sees me waiting for him. The power of a look stops my heart and I think I've rendered him speechless. He hands me my water and I drink, feeling the water run cool down my throat. He sets both glasses on the mantle, never taking his eyes off me. Before any words can be spoken, I'm being led to the sofa.

"Are we done with our games, because I want to give in. You win."

"No, we both win."

He sheds his shirt, then his pants. I lean in to place kisses across his chest while my fingers take advantage of his exposed skin.

He shoves me backwards onto the sofa as I bounce, trying not to giggle too loudly and wake Ben. The only thing left on me is tiny and lacy giving him lots to savor.

"My surprise?"

"No, there's more."

"More?"

I sit up and lean over the top of the sofa, pulling out the little bag from earlier. "This is for you."

He reaches inside and pulls out a box, then opens the lid.

"Is this the watch we saw on our honeymoon?"

"It is. Look at the back."

He reads the engraving.

"My Heart, Forever and Always, Jamie"

Running his thumb over the words, he sets it on the coffee table, slipping his arm around me. He uses his other one to scoot me down flat on the sofa.

"It's perfect. Thank you."

I touch his cheek, feeling the soft stubble on his face, then pull him down to me. "I would give you the world if I could."

He shakes his head. "You are my world. All I need is what I see in these two emerald eyes. Promise me you'll always look at me the way you do now."

As we lay on the sofa wrapped in a throw feeling the coziness of the fire, I snuggle closer to him.

"You do this to me."

"It's my pleasure to do this to you."

I turn to face him as he pulls me in, so I don't fall off the sofa. I feel the soft hair on his chest on my face. He moves his hips closer to me and a smile forms on my lips.

"You've missed me."

*

I've received the results from the DNA testing to prove if I am truly related to Stacey. I waited for Michael to come back from his trip to go over the results, so tonight we'll find out together. Michael returns to the bedroom.

"Tonight I might actually sleep."

"I have the results of the DNA test. I've waited for you to get back before opening it."

He crawls in beside me, wrapping his arm around me. "Why didn't you tell me earlier?"

I turn to him. "I didn't want whatever is inside this envelope to take away from us enjoying each other tonight."

He leans in kissing me. "Hm, for that I am grateful."

I smile up at him. "So am I."

I take in a deep breath, blowing it out. He squeezes my leg. I tear open the letter, but hand it to him. "Will you read it?" Taking the letter from me he begins to read.

"Well?"

"It's true," he says.

The truth wells up heavy inside of me until it spills out of my eyes. I try and smile at him, while wiping the wetness off my face but I fall over into his lap, overcome. His hand rests on my back as he lets me process the information, but I feel his body tense. Sitting up, I see he has tears in his eyes as well. I wrap my arms around him and we support each other in this new finding. He kisses me when I pull away to look up at him.

"Jamie, what are you feeling?"

"I hoped it wouldn't be true, that we didn't share a blood. It makes my heart hurt knowing I'm connected to her forever."

"I'm sorry it turned out this way."

"I'm not crazy like her, am I? I mean, do I exhibit any traits like her at all?"

"No and no. You are sweet, a beautiful woman inside and out with a huge heart. You are passionate about your family, protective, and strong. You are nothing like her and never could be."

I take the paper and toss it off the bed and onto the floor, letting her go. We lie down together with this new information. Michael holds up his hand as I put mine inside his bringing it to my lips.

"I would not have wanted to find this information out with anyone else. I love you."

"I'm with you through this life no matter what. I love you too."

Chapter 32

ight years later…

"Jamie. focus on my voice, you can do this."

"I'm just so tired."

"I know baby, it's been a long time, but they're ready for you to push. Squeeze my hand, let me help you."

"It's coming again." I start my breathing, preparing to push with everything that I have. I grip his hand and focus on his face. He is saving me again. As the baby's head emerges, they say to stop pushing. I lean back as my body takes its last contraction to push out the newest addition to our family.

I look at him, waiting. He's smiling. "It's a girl!"

"Is she okay?"

"Beautiful like her momma." I hear her cry which triggers tears of happiness or exhaustion. I can't quite tell. This little one took two days to make her appearance and I can't wait to hold her.

He cuts the cord and now it's my turn to meet our daughter. They place her on my stomach. Michael bends down to kiss me, then tucks his arm up over my head, leaning on the bed as we look down at our sweet new baby girl.

I hold her close, touching her little face. "Hey you."

Michael touches her arm. "She's small, but those kicks she put in my back during the night were fierce."

"She's a strong girl." I unwrap her. "Look at her."

The nurse comes over to take her. "I'll bring her right back."

I look at my husband. "Are you okay?" I ask. He looks strained.

"It's hard seeing you in that much pain. Two days to get here. You're the strongest person I know."

"You're tired. Thank you for your encouragement and all the back rubs. We put our teamwork into her getting here."

"Yes, we did. I'm going to go check on her. You okay?"

"I am."

As Doctor Rice finishes with me and the nurses clean up around us, I await the numbers on our baby girl.

Michael walks over to me holding a little pink blanket in his arms. "The nurse weighed and measured her. Eight pounds, one ounce. Twenty-one inches long. Good job, Momma."

Everyone's gone, leaving us alone for the first time since delivering our daughter. He's over the top, a proud daddy staying close.

Then the door opens, bringing our first visitors. Harrison comes over to the bed first.

"We've been very worried about you. Everything alright?"

Exhaustion has plowed into me, but this first meeting is important. "Yes, she was just taking her time to make a grand appearance."

"Pink?"

Michael beams. "Yes, a girl."

His dad smiles, looking down at his granddaughter. He kisses my head, then gives Michael a hug, sharing their special moment. There is a commotion at the door.

Michael goes to the door, says a few words, then opens it. Laura comes in with Ben in front of her and holding Jack's hand. Ruby is holding Ethan. Our three boys are about to meet their sister for the first time.

Ruby hands Ethan to Michael. "Congratulations, again."

"Thank you, another Tucker has blessed our family."

She looks at me with concern. "Are you alright? It took a while this time."

"I'm fine, she just wasn't quite ready."

She hugs me, looking down at the baby. "Jamie, she is going to be so spoiled. She's adorable, look at that little nose."

"She's cute, isn't she?"

Laura walks over to the bed eyeing our newest little one when Harrison takes Jack from her. She has tears in her eyes. "How are you both doing?"

"We couldn't be happier."

She lays a kiss on my head then looks at her son, going around the bed to hug him.

"Congratulations dear, I'm so proud of both of you. You have a little girl; how do you feel?"

"Overjoyed." She hugs him again.

Now Ben comes over. "She's cute."

"You're a big brother again, how does it feel?" I ask him.

"Good."

I smile and bring him in for a kiss. He touches the blanket. That's when Jack goes into full on, "Let me see, let me see."

Harrison sits him on the side of the bed, and he gets up on his knees to peek at his sister.

"She's little."

"Yes, but she will be big soon, just like you and both of your brothers."

Michael steps close to the bed with Ethan, who is holding his blanket close to his face, acting a little shy. He lunges towards me as Michael grabs him.

"Hold on buddy, you need to be easy around Momma and the baby."

He sets Ethan down next to me, who crawls over to lay his head on my arm. He reaches over to touch the blanket. The baby moves as he pulls back, looking up at me.

"It's fine, she's waking up."

Ben is the one asking the next important question. "What's her name?"

"Emily."

His face lights up. "It fits her." He looks at Jack. "That's the name we picked."

Jack makes an excited noise, startling Emily as she begins to cry. He draws back with a look of fear that he's done something wrong.

Michael touches his shoulder. "It's all good buddy."

Jack is five years old with brown wavy hair. He is the leap-don't-think kind of kid who keeps us on our toes. Jack loves playing soccer, being outside, and eats everything we give him.

Ben is now nine and protective of his brothers. He loves sports of any kind and wants to be an ethologist and travel to places where animals live in their own habitats. He has a crush on a girl at school, likes watching movies, and his favorite food is pizza.

Ethan is two, quiet and sweet. He loves anything to do with art, dinosaurs, rain boots, and spaghetti. He likes to cuddle up next to me reading books and enjoys spending time with Michael when he plays his guitar.

He whispers in my ear. "She staying?"

"Yes, she is. Will you watch over her when she comes home like your brothers do for you?"

He nods yes.

The door opens as a nurse comes into the room and sees everyone standing around the bed.

"Oh my, welcome everyone. There's a lot of cuteness in this room. How old is everyone?"

Ben speaks up. "I'm nine, Jack is five, and Ethan is two."

"Nice job." She gives him a high five. She looks at me. "How are you doing?"

"I'm good."

She smiles then looks at Michael. "I think Momma needs some food and maybe some rest."

Michael takes over at that point, gathering the boys to tell me goodbye. He takes Ethan who wants to stay with me. Michael gently pats his back and winks at me.

"I'll be right back."

I hate to see them go, but I'm tired, and this little girl is ready to eat. The nurse takes her to check her and to make sure she's all clear of any fluids. She changes Emily's diaper, takes her prints, then wraps her back up for me. She asks me about her name.

"Emily Elizabeth Tucker."

"How pretty, family name?"

"Elizabeth is, the boys picked Emily."

"Can I get you anything? Are you in pain?"

"No, just need to rest."

"I'll be back later. Congratulations, she's a beauty."

"Thank you."

We're now alone in the room. I begin to feed Emily then talk to her. Her little hand lies on my chest.

I've been waiting for you. You are going to be surrounded for life with family that loves you. You will always have someone to count on when you need them. I love you and so does your daddy.

I start to hum the song I've hummed to all my babies, looking into the face of another little Tucker.

Michael returns alone with a bag of food. "I thought you might be hungry for real food."

"I love that you know that. Thank you."

"Did I miss her first feeding?"

"She did great, latched on immediately."

He begins to unpack the bag. "Babe, you look tired. Let me have her, and you take this."

I smell the warm liquid in the bowl. "Chicken noodle, yum."

"The boys love her already. Ethan wanted to know if she could sleep in his bed. When I reminded him of the crib in our room, he was a little disappointed. Ben decided they were to have pizza for dinner, and I told him about the brownie surprises in the cabinet. That made them forget for a bit we were here, and they were going home."

"I heard you speaking with Stan earlier. Do you need to go out of town next week?"

"No, he was able to do it."

"It's working out well that he is a partner."

"Yes, it's a good arrangement."

I stop eating and look over at him. "We have four children."

He laughs. "Yes, we do."

"Are we crazy?"

"Crazy in love is all. We got this. Besides they're shorter than us, rely on us for food and toys, and we have all the keys to the vehicles out of reach."

I giggle, grabbing my abdomen. "This is true."

I watch him carefully hold our daughter. Each child brought out in him an even more protective side. There is nothing he wouldn't do to protect his little Tuckers or me. Our hearts grow bigger with each baby and with each day together. Our lives have turned into madness with a feeling of calm.

"Come lay with me."

"Are you going to behave? I know how much you want me right now."

"I do want you, but we have to wait six weeks, remember."

He lets out a long sigh. "I do."

Pulling Emily close to the bed so we can watch over her, he crawls in beside me. There is nothing I want more than his kind of medicine.

Epilogue

*O*ur lives have been blessed with four children who run around the house, eat all the time, and make us laugh.

Each has a different personality, different likes, and the ability to melt their dad's heart, even when he disciplines them. He does it in a way that lets them know what they did was wrong, but that he still loves them.

Today is Emily's first birthday and everyone is coming over to celebrate. His parents came into town from Alaska last night, and they said jet lag wasn't keeping them from attending her special day.

Ruby brought John with her. They've been together as a couple for two years and I think things are getting serious. She opened a bakery in Texas about a year ago, making all her best recipes and sharing them with everyone. She's in the kitchen putting the finishing touches on Emily's birthday cake.

The doorbell rings, sending two of the boys to the door as their father yells out to stop. They stand back until he gives the okay to open the door.

Susan and Thomas come in with their kids. Madison is four and Jacob is six months. They've been living here in New York since she graduated, allowing our families to be inseparable and the occasional night out on the town for adults only.

Michael sends everyone in as the boys take Madison and Thomas over to the playroom. Susan comes in the kitchen with Jacob.

"I'm about to burst out all over my new blouse if I don't feed him." She kisses my cheek and I give Jacob lots of smiles.

"Tell Mommy it's all good. She's just exaggerating."

I pull him out of the seat, kissing his little cheeks and hand him to her as she sits in a chair and begins to feed her son. Motherhood agrees with her. She decided to give up her job and stay home. Less stress, happy mommy.

I look outside to see Alysse with Emily in the swing as Ethan plays on the slide. Robert catches him as he comes down, playfully throwing him in the air. Savannah stands nearby lovingly watching her kids, as she calls them. Her love and knowledge of how to fit women caught the eye of so many that she turned it into a design/consulting business, which keeps her very busy.

The doorbell rings again and I know it's Caleb. I yell that I got it. When I open the door, he's holding a bag of gifts. When he visits, he doesn't just bring gifts for one Tucker child, he brings one for all.

His wife Ava is trying to wrangle their twins, Matthew and Dylan, when Eli asks where Ben is. Before I can answer, Ben is bouncing down the stairs, taking Eli with him to the backyard.

Ava is holding the twin's hands, but they just want to run and follow the boys. She gives me the "Is it okay?" look and I nod. She turns them loose and they follow the others out the door. She hugs me, looking exhausted, and I make a suggestion.

"I have special drinks for the adults in the kitchen. Help yourself."

A smile appears on her face. "You are an angel."

Caleb closes the door and I smile, welcoming him. "Well hello."

His hug is firm, lifting me off the floor.

"You aren't still trying to sweep my wife off her feet, are you?" Michael asks, grinning.

"No, that train left a long time ago." He extends his hand to Michael. "Good to see you, man. You still have those muscles I see."

"And you have?"

"Good looks."

"Okay boys let's move this party inside," I order.

We all head into the kitchen, hugging and dispersing drinks. After about 20 minutes and when Susan finished breastfeeding, we all go outside to join everyone else.

Michael grabs my hand, pressing me against the wall before joining the others. He's smiling, and I can't help but wonder what he's thinking. He turns his head to look out the window of our back door.

"Look, what do you see?"

"Family, friends, and a whole lot of love."

"This is what we've always talked about. A life full of normal."

"Normal? With four kids, three dogs, and two businesses, this is what makes you happy?"

He tucks a piece of hair behind my ear. "Yes absolutely. We have built a beautiful life for ourselves and I wouldn't change any of it."

I lay my ear on his chest listening to the beat that drives me, comforts me, and gives me the promise of wonderful things ahead.

I look up at him. "I love you for giving me all of this, for believing in us, and loving me with your heart and soul."

"Thank you for giving me those crazy little people out there and showing me what life can be when you are loved so deeply." He pulls me in a little closer, raising his eyebrow and showing me that little glimmer in his eye that has brought those four little ones into this house.

"No, no. What are you thinking?"

"What do you mean?"

"I know that look. It means I'm about to get pregnant."

He pulls something out of his back pocket that piques my curiosity. "Look at them."

To my surprise there are two airplane tickets to the island where we spent our honeymoon.

"Are you serious? How can we do this?"

"The boys are on summer vacation, Emily is a year old. I feel an island trip is in order—clothes optional, of course. It would be just the right thing to do. What do you say?"

"I think you are amazing. Yes, yes let's do it."

I jump up in his arms, kissing him as he kisses me back. There's a little twinge in my belly being so close to him. He sets me down with another kiss. How easy it is to get lost in him, in this feeling. That is, until the door bursts open, bumping into us.

"Oh my God, really?" Caleb demands. "Do you guys ever stop? You do have guests out here who are hungry for food."

We smile at Caleb who grins back. Michael pretends to punch him in the stomach, and he bends over like it was a real punch.

Michael reaches for my hand. "Let's go gorgeous."

He kisses me as we walk out to the family that has seen us through so much. We are truly blessed!

The End

Thank You!

Thank you to my daughter Amy and son Taylor for liking my Instagram post no matter what appears. I love you and you mean the world to me!

Thank you to the ladies who have become a part of "Team Armstrong". Family and friends who take their time to read my books for content, labor over proofreading and lend support when I've needed it. I love you all!

Cheryl, Shirley, Genna, Tieka, Alexis and Ashley

Thanks to Philip Andrews Photography for capturing my vision for the cover.

Thanks to Amy Elizabeth Bishop for editing and making it flow.

Thank you Genna for creating and maintaining my website and connecting all my social media.

A huge thank you to everyone who's read, "My Heart" and will continue with, "Release My Heart".

Look for my upcoming project:
Watermelon Red

Made in the USA
Middletown, DE
31 May 2019